The Case of the Stopped Clock

Other Daniel Marcos Books Are:

The Case of the Phantom Bullet
The Case of the Missing Coffee Pot
The Case of the Sleepy Security Guard
The Case of the Reverend's Son
The Case of the Three Arrests

The Case of the Stopped Clock

From the Case Files of Attorney
Daniel Marcos

Jeffery Sealing

iUniverse, Inc.
Bloomington

The Case of the Stopped Clock
From the Case Files of Attorney Daniel Marcos

This fictional case is based on Colorado Revised Statutes. Therefore, Colorado Law Procedures, Title 16 and the Criminal Code, Title 18, are mentioned or referenced for legal definitions only. Always consult an attorney in all legal cases. The town named is real but no longer exists. The town, for the purposes of this book, was placed outside of Silverton, Colorado for security reasons due to the September 11, 2001 terrorist attacks. Other towns mentioned are real as they are in the counties so named or mentioned.

iUniverse books may be ordered through booksellers or by contacting:

iUniverse
1663 Liberty Drive
Bloomington, IN 47403
www.iuniverse.com
1-800-Authors (1-800-288-4677)

ISBN: 978-1-4759-8623-5 (sc)
ISBN: 978-1-4759-8624-2 (ebk)

Printed in the United States of America

iUniverse rev. date: 04/23/2013

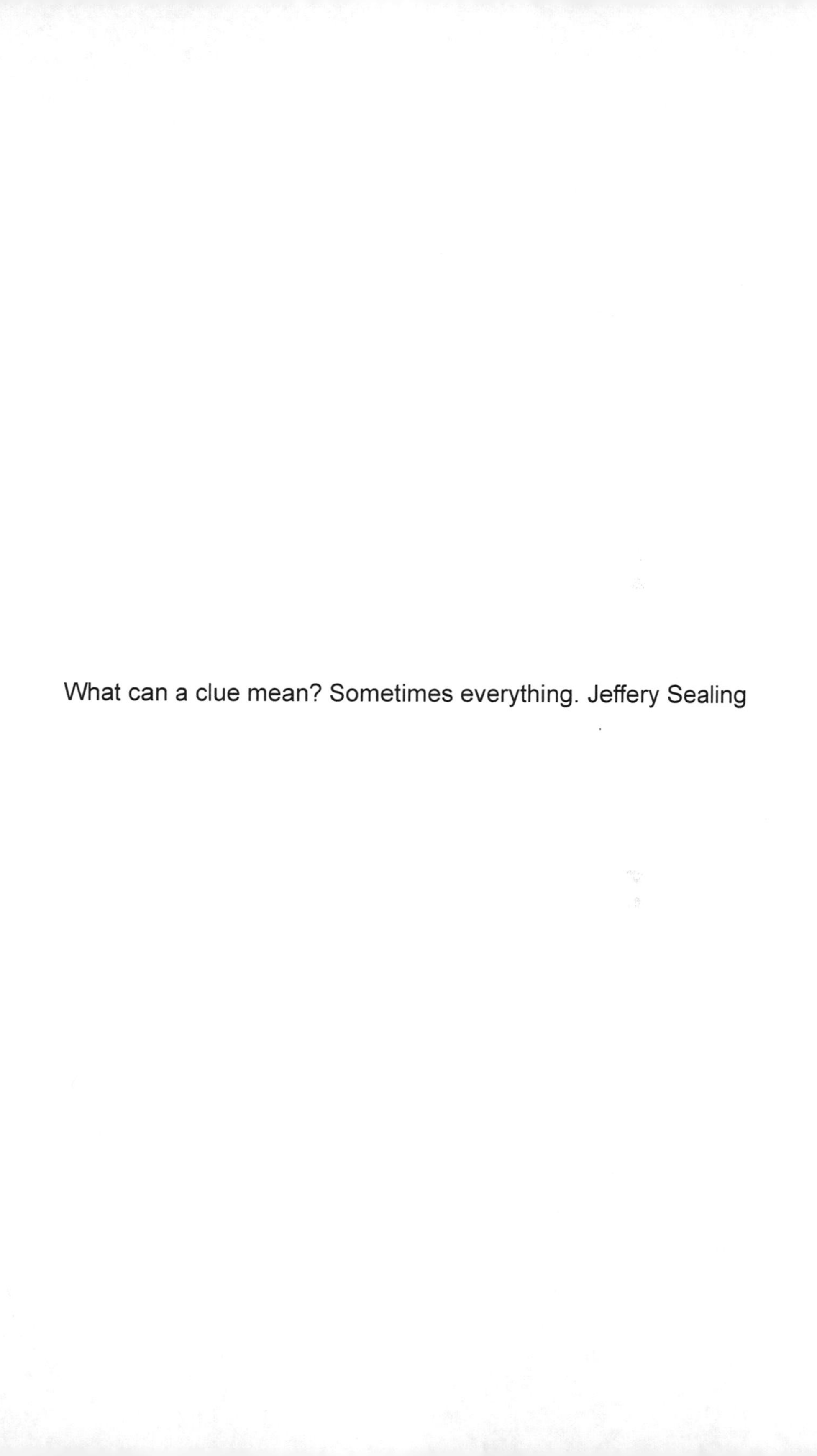

What can a clue mean? Sometimes everything. Jeffery Sealing

CHAPTER 1

Daniel had finished off his last speaking engagement, which was at the Trinidad Community College in Trinidad, Colorado. He had spoken to one of the Criminal Justice classes on Constitutional Law. Daniel went back to his hotel room, packed up his things and checked out of the hotel. He tossed his duffle bag into the trunk of his SUV and stepped into the driver's seat. Once the driver's door was shut, he turned on his cell phone to find he had one missed call from his secretary, Lynn Lyons. He dialed the office number.

"Hello Lynn, what's going on back at the home front?" asked Daniel.

"Linda called about the Davids case. She still wants to charge him with the felony charge of 18-9-116, Throwing Missiles at Vehicles. She's willing to give Mr. Davids probation in lieu of prison time."

"No dice. He may have thrown, or as he told me in his statement at my office, lost control of a rotten watermelon. This rotten watermelon happened to fly over the fence, where he lives at, and exploded, rather nastily, on Miss Dwight's car windshield as she happened to be driving by on her way to her bridge game."

"She still wants to charge him with the felony, Daniel."

"Tell Linda my client will plead guilty to Unlawfully Littering on a Roadway, C.R.S. 42-4-1406 and pay restitution to Miss Dwight for all of her damages. He gets no jail time or probation/parole and will pay the fine in accordance with said statute."

"I don't think she will go for it."

"Then we go to court. She will have to prove malicious intent and willful damage because my client tripped over the garden hose that was in the grass. It was just unfortunate that the garden hose just happened to be the same color as the grass."

"I'll call her back with your counteroffer."

"Good and while you're at it, look up Black's Law Dictionary on the web and find out what is legally defined as a missile and what has to propel the missile, etc.; anything else?"

"On the Smith case, 14CR22, Linda wants to drop the charges against Mr. Smith because the victim doesn't want to press charges."

"Agreed, keep me informed. Send Mr. Smith his final bill and close out the file."

"Yes, Daniel."

Daniel hung up the phone as he pulled up onto Northbound I-25. When he reached the Walsenburg exit, he headed west on Highway 160.

Lynn was busy printing up the legal definition of a missile and stapled all of the paper together. She set the stack of paperwork on Daniel's desk. Next, she called Linda back with Daniel's counteroffer. Linda refused and said she would see Daniel in court the next morning at 10:45am. Lynn passed along the acceptance of case number 14CR22 before she hung up the phone. She was getting ready to lock up the office when Daniel pulled up around 1645 hours.

"Daniel, I wasn't expecting you back until tomorrow," said Lynn, a little surprised.

"Well, I wasn't sure if I would be back before tomorrow either," he replied confidently.

"I printed out the legal definition from Black's Law Dictionary and put it on your desk."

"Looks like it's going to be a long night. Lynn, go on home and I'll see you in the morning."

"Goodnight, Daniel."

Daniel waited until after she had left before locking the doors to the office. He entered his office and turned on the lamp that sat in the middle part of his desk. He stretched out in the chair that was at his desk and picked up the paperwork that Lynn had printed up earlier. After reading over the definition, he called Jessica. Jessica wasn't in her office, so Daniel left her a message to call him as soon as possible. Next, Daniel called Mr. Sean Davids, his client.

"Hello?" said the voice.

"Sean, this is your attorney. We are going to court in the morning at 10:45am. How much money do you have on you?" asked Daniel.

"About $50.00, but I have much more in my savings account at the bank."

"Good. Stop by the bank in the morning and bring $1,000.00 in cash to court with you."

"Okay. Am I going to prison?"

"I seriously doubt it. We are going to be in Courtroom 3, which is Judge Kyle Tillman's court. Dress nicely and be quiet, no matter what is said."

"I will."

Daniel hung up the phone and went home. As Daniel was drifting off to sleep, someone else's day was just starting. At the front gate to the hidden entrance of the Baltimore Testing Center, the nightshift armed Security Officer Bill Berman was running his ID badge through the scanner. The scanner was a cleverly disguised mailbox looking device. When Bill ran his ID badge through the scanner, the scanner produced a number pad under itself. Bill entered his special PIN number and the gate opened for him.

Bill drove into the parking lot and stepped out of his vehicle. As he approached the entrance gate, another employee was just leaving. Bill recognized the employee as Bob Quinest. Bill went to say hello, but Bob stormed right past him. Bill continued through the entrance gate and into the guard shack. He walked into the small office and set his lunch down. As he poured himself a cup of coffee, he started looking over the 2nd shift's log entries. The door opened to the guard shack and the 2nd shift Security Officer, Randy Oliver, entered.

"Good evening, Bill," said Randy.

"Good evening to you as well. Anything exciting going on tonight?" asked Bill as he set the log sheets down on the desktop and sipped his coffee.

"Had some trouble with setting the alarms in the lower labs, but they've been quiet since 2045 hours. Oh, stay out of Lab 3 tonight, the idiots down there are blowing things up again."

They both started laughing. Randy picked up his stuff and left through the front gate entrance. Randy used his exit code on the gate and left the area. As he drove towards Silverton, he passed a car that was parked on the side of the road with no driver in the driver's seat. Randy looked around the area but saw no one anywhere. He dismissed his thoughts of danger as just being tired. He blinked his tired eyes and kept on driving as snow started falling.

The driver of the car had been lying down in the front seat. When Randy had left, they sat up in the driver's seat and started the car. They turned on their headlights and drove towards their former employer's facility. They had decided that their idea was theirs and that no one was going to steal it away from them. They parked their car off to the east side of the main entrance gate.

They put on a black ski mask and black gloves. Carefully they removed all of the rest of the gear they were going to need. They dressed up in more dark clothing and carried their climbing equipment to the front gate. All they had to do was wait for someone to come in or go out and they would be on to the property.

Bill began his nightly routine of filling out paperwork and changing all 22 surveillance cameras' videotapes. He checked the status of the alarm system and saw that it was armed for all but one level; Level 3, which contained labs 3, 3A, 3B and 3C. Bill watched the exterior monitors and the cameras that fed them their pictures. Next, Bill turned off the computer at the desk for a few minutes and then rebooted it. After he had logged into it under his username and unique password, he read his email.

One email was from Barry Goldman, the Chief Security Officer of Rocky Mountain Security Services. The email had been forwarded via Human Resources. The title of the email was simply EMPLOYEE TERMINATION. Bill opened the email and saw that the terminated employee was Bob Quinest. He wondered what Bob had done to get fired. Bill surveyed the rest of his emails and then logged off the computer, shutting it completely down. He went back to drinking his coffee as he watched the snow fall on the exterior cameras.

Julie Halverston, the Assistant Ironton Town Marshal, was sitting in the Ironton Town Marshal's office drinking coffee and going over her arrest paperwork. The three drunken people in her jail were starting to rant and rave again. She put her arrest paperwork down and went over to the door to the cells. She used her keys to open the door a little. She then used her nightstick to pound on the doorframe.

"Everybody shut up in there or I will gas you all!" she yelled.

She shut and relocked the door as the ranting and raving ended. She sat back down at her desk and called the San Juan County Sheriff's Department dispatcher to check-in. She then turned up the volume on the police scanner to listen in on the other departments in the area. The only thing going on so far was a DUI stop on the other side of the county by the Colorado Highway Patrol.

A car pulled up to the gate and the driver swiped his ID badge in the scanner. The scanner asked for the person's special PIN number. The driver punched the code in and the gate opened. The car drove in and as the gate started closing, the figure ran in behind the car and quickly hid behind some garbage cans. The driver of the car parked his car and quickly ran over to the main entrance. Bill looked up when the man used his ID badge in the card reader next to the guard shack. The name that came up was Joe Kapps, Lab Technician, Level 6.

The figure waited until Bill started on his rounds before they started moving out of the shadows. The figure moved about cautiously and was only observed by one of the security cameras. The camera was equipped with not only motion sensing grids in the lens but also infrared heat sensing grids. The camera followed the figure until it reached the limit of its scan capabilities.

The figure, using a stolen ID badge from one of the maintenance personnel, slid the card into the card reader by the door next to the guard shack. The figure entered a random, seven digit PIN number. The computer processed the request and opened the door. The figure moved down the hallway and pressed the elevator call button. When the empty elevator car arrived and the doors opened, the figure tossed their climbing equipment into the car as the doors closed. Working quickly, the figure climbed up the walls of the elevator, popping open the escape hatch.

The figure tossed their climbing equipment up onto the roof of the elevator. The figure carefully closed the roof hatch so no one would suspect anything was wrong or out of place. Next, the figure put on their climbing equipment harness and prepared to wait until the elevator dropped down to Level 6. The figure also knew where and how the mantraps worked.

The figure could avoid them and they planned on waiting until Joe Kapps left before doing their dirty work. The figure was planning on stealing the report on the Portable Laser Cutting Unit that the government didn't want. The figure knew the unit would work well above 10,000 feet/3,333 meters, underwater up to

20-feet/6-meters and was not faulty in its design for safety. The figure began the long waiting process.

Joe Kapps, having poured himself a cup of coffee from one of the coffee makers outside of the closed employee's cafeteria, walked into the elevator and pushed the special access code for Level 6. The figure opened the hatch just enough to see whom it was who had stepped into the elevator; the figure only prayed that it wasn't security. The elevator soon started its descent towards Level 6. The figure closed the hatch and watched as the floors passed by. Finally, the elevator stopped at Level 6.

Joe exited the elevator and started walking towards his small office, which was some 25 yards/8 meters down at the very end of the hallway. The figure waited until the elevator doors had shut before opening the hatch and dropping onto the elevator floor. The figure quickly pushed the "DOORS OPEN" button. The elevator doors opened and the figure stepped out of the elevator. The figure almost walked into the sign at the exit from the elevator.

The sign said, in bold, capital letters, "Warning you are entering a restricted security area. Unauthorized entry or the stealing or willful destruction of any of the documents or materials contained within the premises is illegal. Deadly force is authorized to protect all documents and materials contained within the premises in accordance with Title 18, U.S.C. as Amended, Section 1899."

Since Joe's presence would mean that Joe would have disarmed the security system temporarily, the figure easily stepped over the first mantrap. The figure then quickly ducked down below the level of the windows, which lead to the administrative offices where Joe was sitting at his computer, typing away.

The figure began duck-walking almost to the second mantrap before stopping. He looked around and ducked into the men's room. He checked his equipment once again. The figure estimated that the alarm system wouldn't be activated for about five to seven minutes after Joe left. The figure planned on utilizing this timeframe to access Joe's computer, download the files they needed and then wait again to leave.

Bill had returned from his rounds, did some more paperwork and poured himself another cup of coffee. He reviewed the key card entrances that had been made while he had been on his patrol. Bill saw the usual personnel for the nightshift and then he saw that someone from maintenance was in the facility.

"*That's funny, I didn't get an email from the maintenance supervisor saying that one of his people would be on the property tonight,*" thought Bill to himself.

Bill then reviewed the video logs and saw nothing but snow flying all around on the exterior cameras. The usual personnel moving about on the inside of the facility were shown on the interior cameras for all the active labs at the time. The video logs also showed something dark in color moving about by the main gate. Bill couldn't see any definite shape to the thing, so he figured that it was probably an animal like an elk or bear.

Joe left the facility around 0141 hours. He called the elevator down and shut off the lights. As Joe stepped into the elevator, the figure opened the men's room door a crack to see the elevator doors closing. Now that the area was dark, the figure began moving about. He accessed Joe's computer and copied the files onto a CD. The figure put the CD into one of the many pockets of his climbing jacket he was wearing. As the figure reached the hallway, they tripped off one of the silent alarms on Level 6. The mantraps activated automatically.

Bill's security system alarm monitoring computer went off in his guard shack. Bill turned around to see that the mantraps were activated as well as both the motion and infrared sensors on the cameras were in alarm. Bill saw that the alarms were all coming from Lab 6. He called the alarm monitoring company to report the alarms like he had been trained to do when he was hired. Bill told them that he would check on the alarms and reset the system.

The alarm monitoring company made an entry into their logs and waited.

The figure used his climbing equipment to get past the second mantrap by the administrative offices. As the figure moved towards the elevator, Bill entered the hallway. The figure took out their .25 caliber, semi-automatic pistol and pointed it at Bill. Bill was using his flashlight in the dark hallway; suddenly his flashlight illuminated the figure. Bill could see the figure was pointing something at him.

The figure charged towards Bill, firing several rounds in his direction. Bill was hit in the stomach with one round, yet another round had hit him in the left arm. Bill, now confused, dazed and almost deafened from gunfire in the hallway, drew his service pistol, a Glock® Model 20 with night sights, and started firing at the figure. The figure pushed Bill almost into the mantrap and kicked him in the left arm. Bill almost lost consciousness at that point. As the elevator doors were closing, Bill fired several more rounds. He didn't realize that he had hit the figure in the left ankle.

The figure knew that with the security system activated, the elevator would be locked at the floor of the alarm activation. The figure's ankle was beginning to really hurt them. The figure had planned for getting out of the elevator if the security system had been activated with a motorized rope-climbing device. The figure attached this device to themselves and started "climbing" up the elevator shaft to the very top where maintenance work was done on the elevator. The figure crawled out of the elevator doors and started making their way towards their car.

The figure began packing snow into the bleeding ankle's bullet hole. They finally arrived, limping greatly, at their car. They opened the car door and stepped into their vehicle. The figure pulled out their .25 caliber semi-automatic pistol, inserted a fresh magazine into it, and put it into their lap. The pain from the gunshot wound was getting worse.

Bill woke up and looked around. He saw a dark red spot on the left sleeve of his uniform. He looked at his right arm and then down at his right hand. He still had his Glock® in his right hand. Bill holstered the weapon and tried to stand up. Instantly, he noticed a burning sensation in his right leg. He looked down and saw that he had been hit there as well. Next, he looked around for his flashlight.

He found his flashlight by looking over the edge of the mantrap. There at the bottom of the mantrap was his flashlight. All Bill could do now was wait and hope that someone would find him.

The alarm monitoring company had changed shifts. The oncoming shift noticed that the Baltimore Testing Center was still in alarm. After the outgoing shift had left and the oncoming shift had logged into their computer, they looked at the alarm's times. It had been 22 minutes since the alarms had been activated. He checked to see if the alarms had been reset but they had not been reset. Labs 6A, 6B, 6C, 6D and all of the mantraps were still in alarm.

The alarm technician looked at the alarms and noticed a small heat source in the first mantrap. He then checked the sound recorders and saw that there was a lot of activity on them for 0220 hours in the morning. The alarm technician picked up the phone and called the guard shack first. The phone rang and rang without being answered.

After several repeated attempts to call the guard shack with no response, the alarm technician called the Chief Security Officer, Barry Goldman, of Rocky Mountain Security Services to report the problem. The phone rang three times before a very sleepy Barry Goldman answered his cordless phone.

"This is Barry," he said, yawning.

"I hate to bother you at this hour of the morning, but this is ALS Alarm Monitoring. We currently have all the alarms going off in Lab 6 and all of the mantraps are active. Your security officer doesn't answer the phone, either," said the man.

"When did the alarms start going off?" asked Barry as he took the phone with him into the computer room and turned on all three computers for the Baltimore Testing Center's security system.

"The alarms started going off about 35 minutes ago."

"Thank you, I'll take it from here."

"Goodbye."

Barry logged into the security systems at the facility. He saw the alarms going off in Lab 6 but nowhere else. He tried calling the guard shack but no one answered. Barry then logged into the other parts of the security system and saw that someone from maintenance had used their key card in the key card reader prior to the alarms going off.

"Damn maintenance people, why can't they follow proper policy and procedures like everyone else? Do they think they're special?" Barry said to himself.

He saw that all the mantraps were indeed activated. He checked the elevator's status and found the elevator was locked at Level 6. He then saw a minor heat source in the first mantrap that was at the elevator's exit point. Barry called the guard shack one last time with no answer

Bill looked around and saw that his radio had been shot and was hanging in pieces off of his duty belt. Bill figured he was going to bleed to death down there. He thought about yelling for help, but figured that, although the sound sensors were active and recording, there was no one listening to them at this hour of the morning. Bill put his head down on the cold, steel frame of the mantrap.

CHAPTER 2

Barry called the guard shack several more times without anyone answering. By this time, it was almost 0300 hours in the morning. Barry called the manager on duty in Lab 1. The phone rang only twice before being answered before a woman's voice came on the line.

"Hello and thank you for calling the Baltimore Testing Center, this is Sally, how may I help you?"

"Sally, this is the Chief Security Officer of Rocky Mountain Security Services, Barry Goldman."

"Hello, Barry, how are you doing?"

"Not good, Sally. When was the last time you saw my security officer tonight?"

"About 12:30am or 12:45am."

"Thank you, Sally. Is there anything odd going on at the facility tonight?"

"Yeah, the passenger elevator is stuck on Level 6 and it's snowing very heavily."

"Thank you, Sally. Listen closely; I want you to discreetly gather all of the nightshift personnel into the employee's cafeteria. Have them all put their hands on the tabletops; law enforcement is on their way. Keep everyone in the cafeteria. No one goes anywhere for any reason unless law enforcement or myself tells them otherwise."

"Okay. What about Jared in the wheelchair in Lab 5?"

"Use the handicap elevator. When you swipe your key card, enter the PIN number 0911."

"Okay; goodbye."

Barry hung up the phone and called the San Juan County Sheriff's Department's non-emergency phone number. The dispatcher answered the phone; the time was now 0305 hours.

"Good morning, San Juan County Sheriff's Department. Agent Dell speaking. How can I help you?"

"Agent Dell, my name is Barry Goldman. I'm the Chief Security Officer for Rocky Mountain Security Services. I have a situation in progress at my facility. This facility is located at 18501 west highway 550A."

"What kind of a situation, sir?" he asked as he started typing the information being given to him for broadcast.

"I have alarms going off in a restricted area at the facility which is to be defended by deadly force. I have had no contact with my security officer for over three hours. I have to assume either a medical emergency or a hostage situation."

"Is your security officer armed or unarmed?"

"Armed."

"Okay. Are there any weapons at this facility other than your security officer's?"

"There are four semi-automatic shotguns and four semi-automatic rifles at the guard shack, locked up and lots of ammunition. In Lab 5, there is an armory and shooting range. Lab 3 has explosives, more weapons, landmines and rockets. I also know that at least four of the nightshift personnel have CCW's."

"Thank you, sir. Is there anything else that the responding personnel need to know?"

"Yes. Tell the responding deputy to run their law enforcement ID card through the card reader on the right side. When the computer asks for their PIN number, have them enter 0911."

"Yes, sir; please continue."

"I have instructed the nightshift manager on duty, Sally, I don't recall her last name, to have everyone gathered in the employee's cafeteria with their hands on the tabletops. I do have a disabled employee who may have locked himself in Lab 5. If that is the case, then that's okay; he's completely safe in there."

"Thank you, sir; continue."

"When the deputy gets to the main entrance to the facility which is next to the guard shack, have them swipe their law enforcement ID card again and enter PIN number 0911."

"Okay, continue, sir," he said as he typed in all of the information and put it out on flash traffic to the responding deputy, the Ironton Town Marshal's Office, the Silverton Town Marshal's Office and the Colorado Highway Patrol.

"When the deputy gets to the elevator at the end of the hallway from the guard shack, have them swipe their ID card again while holding down the elevator call button for at least 30-seconds."

"Okay, sir, please continue."

"Have them enter the PIN number 2468. That will temporarily override the security system and bring the elevator to the main floor. When the deputy gets into the elevator, have them push 6, 5, 6, 6 in that order on the floor selection panel. The elevator should take them directly to Level 6 and Lab 6."

"Thank you, sir. Is there anything else we should know?"

"Nothing right now. However, I am enroute to the facility and if anyone has any questions, they can call my cell phone number, 970-646-9797."

"Thank you, sir."

Barry dressed and headed out the door towards his facility. By 0350 hours, the San Juan County Sheriff's Department Deputy, Gilda Hold, the Assistant Silverton Town Marshal, Bob Biss, the Colorado Highway Patrol, Trooper Davis and the Assistant Ironton Town Marshal, Julie Halverston were on scene. By the time Barry arrived at 0445 hours, Bill Berman was being taken away in an ambulance to Durango for the treatment of his gunshot wounds.

After the crime scene crew processed the scene in Lab 6, Barry went to his office to await any word on what had happened. He called the CEO, CFO, CIO, COO and the CLO of the company to tell them what had happened.

"Barry, what's going on at the facility?" asked the CEO who had put Barry on a speakerphone so that the board could listen to the conversation.

"I have a security situation at the facility. Per this particular security situation and in accordance with company policy and procedures, I am implementing Security Procedure 29. I am requesting that immediate disaster recovery plan Charlie be implemented."

The CEO looked around at the other board members who nodded their heads in agreement.

"The board agrees for right now. What facts do you have at this time?" asked the CIO.

"I have only three facts so far. Fact one, an unknown entity or entities broke into the facility sometime after midnight. Fact two, this entity or these entities then broke into Lab 6. Fact three, when my security officer went to check on the alarms that were going off, this entity or these entities shot my security officer. I have ascertained that he did return fire."

"How is he doing?" asked the CLO.

"Just fine. He is semi-conscious and has non-life threatening wounds to his right leg and left arm. One of the bullets did destroy his radio; that is why he couldn't call for help."

"We will prepare a statement for the company and its employees. I will call the department head for Lab 6 and tell him to keep his people out of the lab until further notice," said the CEO.

"Thank you, madam."

"Keep the board informed of any developments," said the CEO as she hung up the phone.

Daniel was walking into courtroom 3 with his client. Sean went directly to his chair at the Defendant's table. As Daniel was walking past the first row of spectator's benches, Miss Dwight stood up and spoke to Daniel.

"You're such a nice young, muscular man for an attorney," she said, winking her right eye at him and smiling widely.

"Why, thank you, Miss Dwight. By the way, what were your damages for the accident?" asked Daniel nicely.

"About $650.00; good luck, counselor," she said coyly.

Daniel turned around just as Linda was walking past him. Linda proceeded to her table and started shuffling around paperwork. Daniel suddenly felt his left buttocks being pinched. He pursed his lips together and sat down at his table. Linda leaned over to speak to Daniel.

"Last chance, counselor," she said.

"No dice, here's your paperwork," he replied, handing Linda the paperwork from last night.

"Thank you, counselor. By the way, don't speak to any of the victims in any more of my cases, or I will have you disbarred."

"Your victim spoke to me first, counselor. No Miranda violation for the Res Gestae statements that the victim makes to legal counsel; attorney/client privileges."

"I see."

The door to the left side of the courtroom opened and Sergio stepped forward to address the court properly. Everyone stood up even before Sergio started speaking because they knew the routine.

"All rise. Criminal court in the case of *The People V. Sean Davids,* case number 13CR19, is now in session. The Honorable Judge Kyle Tillman, presiding," said Sergio.

"You may be seated. This is only a preliminary hearing," said Judge Kyle Tillman as he sat down at his bench and put on his glasses so he could read over the paperwork.

Everyone sat down.

"Is the victim present?" asked Judge Kyle Tillman.

"I am, Your Honor," replied Miss Dwight, waving her right hand.

"Is the defendant present?"

"I am, Your Honor," said Sean, standing up and then sitting back down.

"Is defense counsel present?"

"I am, Your Honor. It's good to be back in your courtroom and to see you."

"Likewise, counselor. Is the prosecution present?"

"The People are present, Your Honor."

"Very well. Prosecution, proceed with your statements of the facts in this case."

"Your Honor, on September 18th of 2013, the defendant did purposefully and willfully throw a rotten watermelon at the victim's car windshield. The rotten watermelon impacted the windshield, exploding violently. This caused the victim to lose control of her car because she couldn't see. The victim said, in her statement to me in my office, she thought she had hit someone, killing them. Therefore, The People are charging the defendant with the felony offense of 18-9-116, Throwing Missiles at a Vehicle."

"So noted; defense counsel?"

Daniel stood up and began to speak.

"Boy, with an opening statement like that, my client must be guilty as charged for the crime. Your Honor, my client had a simple accident. There are no true witnesses to the crime, albeit except for the victim. There are no accomplices and certainly no pre-meditation on the part of either my client or the rotten fruit to commit this felony offense."

The courtroom started chuckling at that comment. Judge Kyle Tillman banged his gavel down several times and the courtroom quieted down.

"I have a copy of the legal definition of a missile. My client, Your Honor, was merely taking the rotten fruit out to the garbage can which was located at the curb at his residence."

"Just a minute, counselor, does the prosecution and this court have this legal definition of a missile?" interrupted Judge Kyle Tillman.

"I have provided the prosecution with a copy of said definition. Your Honor may have my copy as defense Exhibit A," said Daniel, handing his copy to Sergio.

"So noted; bailiff please bring me the defense counsel's paperwork. Do you have any objections, prosecution, at this being entered as evidence?"

"The People have no objections, Your Honor."

"So noted."

Judge Kyle Tillman marked the copy then went back to listening to the case.

"You may proceed again, counselor."

"Thank you, Your Honor. My client tripped over the garden hose that was in the grass and the rotten watermelon flew out of his hands. Miss Dwight just happened to be driving by at the same time," said Daniel as he used his left hand to point to the victim.

"Very well. The prosecution may call its first witness," said Judge Kyle Tillman.

"The People call the first and only witness in the case to the witness stand, Miss Dwight," said Linda.

After Miss Dwight had taken the stand, Sergio swore her in. Miss Dwight waited for Linda's questions. After Linda had asked only a few questions, Daniel was able to get up to speak to her on the witness stand.

"Miss Dwight, you were going up the street to your weekly bridge game, right?" asked Daniel.

"Yes, I was. You've got a nice butt, counselor," she said, smiling widely again.

The courtroom started laughing at the statement she had made. Judge Kyle Tillman had to bang his gavel down several times before speaking.

"Quiet in this courtroom or I will have it cleared. The witness will refrain from making personal comments about defense counsel's body parts outside of defense counsel's questions.

Is that clear, Miss Dwight?" asked Judge Kyle Tillman, almost laughing himself.

"Yes, I understand, Your Honor. But it is the truth."

"Thank you for the compliment, Miss Dwight. Miss Dwight, when you lost control of your car from the impact on the windshield of the alleged missile, how much damage was caused?" asked Daniel, smiling at her.

"Let's see. I ran into a parked car and my nerves were shot for a few days."

"I see. Do you know how much damage was done to the parked car?"

"About $500.00."

"Okay. Were you seen by your doctor, the emergency room doctors, anybody like that?"

"Yes, my doctor saw me that afternoon at his clinic in Silverton."

"Thank you and did your doctor prescribe any medications for you to take?"

"Yes, he did give me a prescription for some pills that really did a number on me, I'll tell you."

"Great. Now, how much did all of that cost you?"

"About $150.00."

"So my client cost you about $650.00 in damages, is that right?"

"Yes, I guess so."

"Thank you, Miss Dwight. No more questions of this witness, Your Honor."

"The witness is excused. This court is in recess until 1:00pm," said Judge Kyle Tillman, banging his gavel down.

"All rise," said Sergio as Judge Kyle Tillman left the courtroom.

After the lunch break, court reconvened. Judge Kyle Tillman looked down at both counsels.

"Is the prosecution ready with closing arguments in the case?" asked Judge Kyle Tillman.

"The People are ready, Your Honor. The People feel that they have proved their case. The defendant is guilty of the charge," said Linda as she looked over at Daniel.

"So noted. Defense counsel, are you ready with your closing arguments?" he asked.

"Defense is ready, Your Honor," said Daniel without looking at the judge.

"Proceed."

"Your Honor, my client had a simple accident; nothing more, nothing less. There was no purposeful intent in this accident my client had. He didn't get up that morning, deciding that at 10:45am, he was going to cause Miss Dwight problems by hiding in the bushes. Then my client was going to willfully throw a piece of rotten fruit at Miss Dwight as she drove by," said Daniel.

He paused before continuing.

"No, my client did none of those things. There was no conspiracy, or complicity either, on the part of my client, the garden hose or the rotten fruit. It is unfortunate that Miss Dwight just happened to be driving by when the rotten fruit was lobbed at her car windshield like a grenade."

Daniel paused once again.

"Furthermore, my esteemed colleague, Linda here, has failed to adequately prove that my client threw, on purpose, an alleged missile. She has failed to prove conspiracy or complicity on the part of my client, the rotten fruit, the garden hose or Miss Dwight to cause my client to throw an alleged missile. She has also failed to prove that a rotten, stinking piece of fruit meets the legal definition of a missile. Defense requests a dismissal of the charges and rests, Your Honor."

"Very well. Does the prosecution have any rebuttal arguments?" asked Judge Kyle Tillman.

"Only one, Your Honor. All Colorado Revised Statutes requires me to prove is that an object, which I define as a missile, did in fact strike the windshield of Miss Dwight's car, causing her to lose control of her car. This loss of control of the car caused property damage to the victim, another person and caused the victim to have to seek medical treatment for her injured nerves. And no, Your Honor, The People will not go for a dismissal of the charges."

"So noted. This court is in recess until I've had a chance to review defense counsel's evidence and make some phone calls."

"All rise," said Sergio as Judge Kyle Tillman left the courtroom.

The courtroom was quiet. Linda and Daniel started discussing other cases while Sean walked around outside the courtroom. Daniel was drinking a cup of tea and Sean had just come back into the courtroom. Sean had sat down as Daniel looked up at the clock on the wall to the left of where the judge sits. The time was 1645 hours. Sean turned to face Daniel.

"What's taking so long, Daniel?" asked Sean, nervously.

"I'm doing the job you paid me to do; defend you. I've got the judge and the spectators all thinking. Just sit back and relax."

"I'll try."

At 1655 hours, Sergio stood up from his desk as Judge Kyle Tillman entered the courtroom.

"All rise, criminal court is back in session in the case of *The People v. Sean Davids,* case number 13CR19. The Honorable Judge Kyle Tillman, presiding," he said.

"Be seated. Will the defendant and his defense counsel please rise," said Judge Kyle Tillman.

Daniel and Sean stood up.

"In the case of *The People v. Sean Davids,* case number 13CR19, this court, after carefully reviewing the evidence supplied by defense counsel and a conference call with the Colorado State Attorney General, finds that a piece of rotten fruit does not meet the legal definition of a missile."

He paused before continuing.

"This court must also side with defense counsel for dismissal of the charges provided that Mr. Davids pays restitution to the victim in the amount of $650.00, pays all court costs and defense counsel is requested to have coffee with the victim, Miss Dwight, tomorrow morning at 7:00am at her place. This case is dismissed," he said, banging down his gavel.

"Agreed, Your Honor," said Daniel as he shook hands with Sean and pointed him in the direction of the clerk of the court's office to pay the restitution and court costs.

"See you tomorrow, counselor," said Miss Dwight, winking her left eye at Daniel.

"I'm looking forward to it, Miss Dwight," replied Daniel.

As everyone left the courtroom, Daniel ran into Lynn. Lynn handed him his only message. He read the message and pulled out his cell phone to call his friend, Barry Goldman.

"Daniel, what a pleasant surprise," said Barry.

"Barry, good to hear from you. It's been about seven years since we last saw or spoke to each other, hasn't it?"

"Yeah; college graduation. Look, I need a favor from you."

"What do you need?"

"What's your rate and when can you start?"

"My rate is $485.00 an hour, minimum ten hour retainer and I can start tonight if you need me to."

"Thank you and I want you to stop by your client's house in Silverton. I gave your secretary the address; goodbye."

Barry hung up his cell phone as Daniel hung up his. Daniel looked over at Lynn with a very perplexed look on his face.

CHAPTER 3

Daniel woke up at his usual time of 0500 hours. He stretched before working out. He showered, ate breakfast and left his house. He headed out to have coffee with Miss Dwight as had been ordered. He pulled into the curb in front of her house and stepped out of his car. He walked up the sidewalk to her front door and he rang the doorbell; the time was 0655 hours. She opened the door.

"Good morning, counselor, coffee will be ready shortly; please come inside," she said.

"Why, thank you, Miss Dwight and a good morning to you as well," said Daniel, smiling, as he walked inside of her house, shutting the door.

Daniel looked around her living room. There were antiques all over the room. He saw a chess set, which was located in the right corner of the living room next to a wide, five-shelf bookcase. This chess set appeared to be made almost of solid gold with an inscription of "18 of 20" on the side plate. He looked over at the wall to his left and saw several literary awards with pictures of a young woman accepting the awards from the awarder. He knew in an instant that the woman pictured was Miss Dwight.

Daniel turned around to his right to see that the large bookcase was filled up with hardback edition books. Daniel grabbed one of the books at random and looked it over briefly. There in print was the name of the author; E. Dwight. Daniel skimmed through the book, putting it back into the bookcase where it had come from when Miss Dwight entered the room.

"Coffee is ready, counselor," she said as she entered the kitchen.

"Thank you. You're a romance writer, aren't you, Miss Dwight?" asked Daniel.

"What makes you think that, counselor?" she asked as she poured the coffee and handed Daniel a cup.

"There are 47 books on the bookshelf all with your last name on them. Does the 'E' stand for Ellie or Ezra?" he asked, taking the cup of coffee she had handed him.

"Ezra, counselor. Your powers of deduction are impressive," she said as she stared at his chest.

"Do you play chess?" asked Daniel as he sat down at the kitchen table.

"Not much, recently. Years ago, I had regular chess matches with a woman from Durango every Wednesday; she passed away two years ago. I haven't found a worthy opponent to play against, up here."

"Might I suggest my former client, Mr. Davids? He is the Silverton High School Chess Champ three years running."

"A worthy opponent indeed, counselor."

"Those literary awards, what years?" asked Daniel as he drank more of the coffee.

"1965, 1969, 1974 and 1980."

"Historical Romance?" asked Daniel, after having thought about the book he had skimmed through earlier.

"Yes, again, counselor; your powers of deduction are most impressive."

"Do you still write?"

"I stopped writing in 1981. Sold my first novel for $100.00. Sold my last novel for $15,000.00. Counselor, do you pump iron?" she asked as she licked her lips and stared at his chest.

"Yes, I do. Every morning from 0500 to 0545 hours."

What does this old bat want with me? thought Daniel.

"It shows. Counselor, would you take your shirt off, please?" she asked nicely.

"Sure."

Daniel stood up, loosened his tie and pulled it off over his head. He set the tie down on the tabletop. Daniel took off his suit jacket he had been wearing. He put his suit jacket over the back of the chair that he had been sitting in just a few minutes earlier. He then unbuttoned his shirt and took it off. Daniel flexed his chest and arm muscles for her.

"What a body, counselor and you're a Native American, as well," she said as she started to pant.

"Why, thank you, Ezra and yes, I am Native American," he replied.

She smiled and passed out at the kitchen table in her chair. Daniel finished off his coffee, putting his work shirt and tie back on. He then made sure that she was still breathing before he left.

Daniel drove to Bill Berman's place to check on him. When Daniel arrived at Bill's place, the door was already open and he could hear voices inside. Daniel knocked on the doorframe. Bill answered the door, on crutches and trying to remain civil. He hobbled around enough to let Daniel into his small apartment.

"How long have you been here, Bill?" asked Daniel.

"About an hour and I find these guys ransacking my place!" Bill yelled.

"Relax, Bill. Did these men give you a business card saying whom they were or serve you with a search or seizure warrant; anything like that?"

"Yes, they gave me this business card," said Bill, handing Daniel the business card.

Daniel looked over the front of the business card. The men were from the Denver, Colorado office of the FBI. Daniel turned the card over and saw that there was a case number written on the back. Daniel committed the number to memory until he could write it down later. He gave the business card back to Bill as the men left the apartment. Daniel could see one of the men holding three plastic evidence bags. The other man looked at Bill and smiled.

"Hope you have a good attorney," he said.

Daniel tapped the man on the left shoulder.

"He does, he has me and I will advise him of his Constitutional rights if need be," replied Daniel, reaching into his right, inside suit jacket pocket, handing the man his business card.

"Attorney Daniel Marcos, Esquire, should've known," said the man, disgustedly, as he left with his partner.

After Daniel had closed the door, he turned to face Bill.

"I thought I recognized your face, sir," said Bill, shaking Daniel's left hand.

"Why, thank you, Bill. Barry is an old friend of mine and he asked me to stop by and see how you were doing. Looks like I arrived just in time."

"They just can't come in here like that and do what they did, can they?"

"Unfortunately, yes, they can, courtesy of phase III of the USA PATRIOT ACT. However, I think I can get your property back. The judge listed on the back of the business card is a friend of mine," he said, handing Bill another business card.

"Am I a criminal now?" Bill asked as he took the business card.

"Has anyone arrested you, charged you with a crime or interrogated you, yet?"

"No, not yet."

"You're safe for now, then. When are you allowed to go back to work?"

"Monday."

"Do you have a copy of the doctor's orders, recommended therapies and treatments, etc.?"

"Yes."

"Good, keep all of it handy. I just might be able to make the person who shot you, pay for everything. If you need me, I'll be at my office. After hours, don't hesitate to call the emergency number listed on the card."

"Thank you, sir."

Daniel left Bill's apartment and arrived at his office with a big smile on his face. He took off his suit jacket and hung it up on the coat rack in the office. He then walked over to the coffee pot and poured himself a cup of coffee. Daniel noticed that Lynn had been watching him suspiciously since he had entered the office.

"Well, how did your coffee date go?" asked Lynn, sarcastically.

"The date went very well," replied Daniel, smiling from ear to ear.

"Did you have sex with her?" asked Lynn, almost laughing at what she had asked.

"Absolutely not, Lynn. All she asked me to do was take off my shirt. When I did, she passed out in her chair at the kitchen table. She was alive and breathing when I left her."

"I'll bet."

"Lynn, if I had sex with that charming woman, Linda would be over here in a minute. She would arrest and charge me with Manslaughter 18-3-104, Subsection A, recklessly causing the death of another. Linda would then argue in court that the weapon used to kill Miss Dwight was sexual intercourse."

"How could she prove that sex was the weapon of choice?" asked Lynn, almost ready to burst out laughing.

"Linda would argue that I should have known that the woman may have had a heart condition and that something strenuous, in this case, sex, would cause her death. They call it criminal vicarious liability in law school."

Lynn and Daniel both started laughing. Daniel went through his phone messages. He had one message from a woman named Lidia. The phone number listed was 213-858-9655. This number was part of the Los Angeles City and County lockup area known as Number Five.

"Lynn, do you know what this Lidia person wanted?" he asked.

"No, all she said was that it was important and that she had been in one of your Constitutional Law classes in La Junta, I think," replied Lynn.

"Okay," replied Daniel as he dialed the number and a frantic woman's voice answered the phone.

"Mr. Marcos, are you licensed to practice law in the State of California?" said Lidia frantically, almost ready to cry.

"Yes, I am. My California Bar License number is CA1226664DM; what's going on?" asked Daniel, noting the high stress level she was under in her voice.

"My friend and I were arrested for murder. Her for killing the boy and me for being an accessory; they can't do that, can they?"

"Well, a lot depends on the circumstances. Lynn," said Daniel as he placed his right hand over the mouthpiece of the telephone receiver.

"Yes, Daniel," she replied, unconsciously grabbing a legal pad and pen out of the top drawer of her desk.

"Get in here with a legal pad and get ready to take a statement from a client over the phone," said Daniel, loudly.

Lynn rushed into Daniel's office with the legal pad and pen. Daniel pressed the "SPEAKER" button on the phone.

"Lidia, you're on speaker phone with my secretary, Lynn. She is a paralegal and will be taking notes; is that okay with you? Also, do you swear or affirm that what you are about to tell me is, to the best of your knowledge, the truth, the whole truth and nothing but the truth?"

"Yes, I swear that what I am about to tell you is the truth. I don't have much time on this phone."

"Briefly tell me what happened."

"I flew out to California to see a friend for spring break. She flew in to LAX after she had completed some training in Las Vegas, Nevada, I think. We met these guys our own age that we thought were great. Well, they turned out to be not so great."

"I understand; go on." Daniel looked over at Lynn to see if she had kept up with the conversation. Lynn nodded her head up and down stating that she was ready for more of the story.

"Well, they gave us some fruity drinks of some kind. After the third one, neither my friend nor I were feeling very well. I felt really dizzy and disoriented."

"That statement you just made sounds to me like exposure to either Ketamine® or GHB. I assume then that some sort of an attack took place somewhere remote, right?"

"Yes, you're very good, counselor."

"I'm assuming that after the attack, you both were either taken or went to a local hospital?"

"Yes."

"I'm going to assume that emergency room personnel followed proper policies and procedures in a case like this and did either urine or blood tests on you and your friend, or a rape kit, right?"

"Both, counselor. You are very good, sir. That rape kit was a little unnerving, though."

"I can understand the feeling. Something tells me that the detective may have your toxicology results. I will wager a guess that the results show the post-cursors to either GHB or Ketamine®."

"I'll ask the detective when he gets back. Anyway, these two boys started choking us out. It was a very terrifying experience to be choked out like that. I don't remember much except that the boy who was choking me out was laughing the whole time."

Lynn was starting to have trouble keeping up with the woman, so Daniel stalled her a little.

"Could you wait a minute, I think the mail carrier is coming into the office. I'll have to put you on hold, is that okay?"

"Yeah, sure."

Daniel put her on hold for a few minutes before returning to the conversation.

"Go ahead, Lidia."

"I turned to look at my friend when I heard a bang, sharp and loud. It was then that I passed out."

"Do you remember anything else?"

"Yes, the boy who choked me out lowered me to the ground. By the time I was starting to wake up, the police were there. They took us all, including the boy my friend shot, to the same hospital. We all had the same trauma room with the little curtain dividers."

"I know what you're talking about. What happened next?"

"I remember a lot of yelling from the emergency room staff. The next thing I know, the boy my friend shot died right there."

"Did you see your friend's gun?"

"Yes, the police officer who took all of the evidence from the crime scene showed it to me. The police officer asked me if the gun was the boy's, my friend's or mine. I told them I thought it was my friend's and that's when they, the police, charged me with being an accessory to the crime of murder and her with the murder of the boy."

"Have you fully cooperated with the police and anyone else who has interrogated you?"

"Yes. How could someone die from one gunshot wound?"

"Something tells me that the bullet entered somewhere near the middle, bottom section of the ribcage and may have broken off the Xyphoid Process, forcing it into the liver, causing death. I'll bet the bullet continued on its course into the outer wall of the heart by riding up the bottom side of the sternum."

"What are we going to do about this situation?"

"Well, first off, remain calm, despite what the police or DA do to you and your friend. Second, I'm going to get you good legal representation. All I ask is that you not release any more information until a lawyer by the name of Tom Tomlinsin is present. Can you do that for me?"

"Okay."

"By the way, is your friend a police officer of some kind? Because the State of California doesn't recognize any other state's CCW permits, nor is it easy to get a CCW for the State of California."

"Yes. I think she told me one time that she works for the Idaho Department of Revenue as an Alcohol Enforcement Agent."

"That's good information for the both of you. Do you want me to advise you of your Constitutional rights?"

"No, the detective so far hasn't been ugly with me."

"Very well, Mr. Tomlinsin will be in touch with you and your friend, shortly," said Daniel as he hung up the phone.

"Lynn, get all that information typed up and call Tom Tomlinsin in LA. Tell him that I am calling in my favor from a few years ago for these nice ladies."

"Will do; anything else?"

"Not at the moment."

Bob Quinest was waiting nervously at his apartment for the man on the phone to show up. He wasn't feeling well and hoped that this feeling would go away soon. Bob was starting to sweat, had developed some minor twitching and now hot and cold flashes were occurring. He looked down at his left ankle that had been shot by the security guard.

The ankle was badly swollen and now Bob noticed some puss-like discharge coming from the bullet hole. The bullet had shattered his ankle and passed on through into the elevator wall. He hobbled around inside his apartment when there came a knock at the door. Cautiously, Bob hobbled over to the door and opened it only a crack. He could see a man standing there through the haze of his eyes that were blurry.

"Bob, could you open the door a little further?" asked the man.

"Sure, come on inside," said Bob as he opened the door to let the man inside. Bob then closed the door.

As the man walked into the living room, he looked down at Bob's left ankle. The man was holding a briefcase, which he set down on the living room tabletop.

"Are you all right?" asked the man.

"Yeah, I just twisted my left ankle a few days ago."

"Terribly sorry about that. Maybe you should come work for us after all. We do have great medical, dental and vision plans and really nice weather in the Miami, Florida area."

"I just might do that, but industrial espionage is still illegal."

"Yes, but it is very profitable," said the man as he opened up the briefcase to show the money to Bob.

"It's all there like I asked?" said Bob as he coughed while wiping sweat from his forehead with a handkerchief.

"Just liked you asked. $650,000.00 in cash, used $50 and $100 bills. As you requested, no sequential numbering of the bills."

"Great and here's what you paid for," said Bob as he handed the man the CD.

"Thank you and I assume that all the information is there?"

"Yes, it is. Besides, if I tried to cheat you, you would probably have me killed."

"Smart man, have a good day and it was a pleasure doing business with you," said the man as he shook Bob's left hand.

"You as well, sir."

The man left as Bob began counting the money. As the night wore on, Bob began to have convulsions. He looked down at his left ankle and noticed red streaks radiating out from there up his leg. Bob then noticed the smell. He winced as the stench from his left ankle reached his nose. At 1938 hours, Bob's convulsing body lay still in his bed.

The clock on Bob's former desk at his former workstation stopped at that exact time. Nobody but Joe in Lab 6 that night even noticed something was amiss. Joe thought it was nothing more than a dead battery in the clock. He merely put in a maintenance request for a new battery. It was a Wednesday night and the wind was blowing slightly. Back at Bob's apartment, all five clocks had also stopped at the same time; 1938 hours.

The strange man, whom had been in Bob's apartment the day before he died, was stepping off of a private plane in south Florida.

The man waited for the pilot to secure the ladder before exiting the plane. As the man stepped off the plane and onto the tarmac, a helicopter landed. The man stepped aboard the helicopter and it took off. Forty minutes later, the helicopter landed on the roof of a high-rise in downtown Fort Lauderdale, Florida.

The man waited until the pilot opened the passenger door. He quickly exited the helicopter and headed for the exit from the roof. The helicopter took off, disappearing into the nighttime sky. As the man opened the roof exit door, the owner of the building could be seen in the moonlight. Innovative Energy Systems, Inc. The man closed the door, scanned his ID card into the security scanner and walked down twelve flights of stairs.

The door to the bottom of the stairwell at level one was secured by another security scanner and maglock. The man scanned his ID badge again, punched in a special access code and waited. The door's magnetic lock snapped open and the man was able to enter the executive suites. The man continued walking down the hallway until he came to a door with a light coming out from under it. He knocked on the door and it opened up automatically. He entered the office of the Chief Executive Officer of the company, Doug Allison.

"Good evening, Aaron. I heard the helicopter approach and I trust you have what I sent you to get?" he asked.

"Yes, Doug, all the information is on this CD," replied Aaron as he dropped the CD on Doug's desktop.

"I trust that you had no problems with the payoff?"

"None; tell Dave, the CFO, thank you for his assistance."

"Will do. Why don't you go down to the company's gym and workout while I review the information?"

"Okay."

Aaron disappeared and an hour and half later returned to Doug's office. Doug was smiling from ear to ear. Doug stood up and handed Aaron a set of car keys.

“What are these for, Doug?” asked Aaron as he took the car keys from Doug.

“Your bonus for getting the Board of Directors the information I told them I could get. I had the car brought down by train from the New York City dealership this morning when you phoned me; goodnight.”

Aaron almost ran out of Doug’s office heading for the parking garage. There on the first level of the parking garage, parked in a visitor’s parking space, was his dream car; the Mercedes-Benz McLaren in black with the V-10 engine.

CHAPTER 4

Barry was sitting at his desk when Laura, the Chief Information Officer, stepped inside his office. She closed the door and locked it before handing Barry the report he had asked for about a week ago. Barry read the report and then set it down on his desktop.

"Good work, Laura. It appears that only one file was accessed in Lab 6," said Barry.

"Thank you, Barry and I'm sorry that it took this long to get the information to you. Sometimes computers don't always cooperate with their human operators very well. The file that was accessed wasn't accessed in the normal sense. Someone made a copy of it and, I would guess, put it onto a CD or DVD."

"Well, someone had to access the computer system to get the item."

"True. Barry, I assume that your security officers don't have access to the labs do they?" she asked.

"No. They only have access to the main doors and corridors to the labs. They only have full access to Labs 1 through 5 except when Lab 3 is doing destructive testing. What do you make of the file that was accessed?"

"If I didn't know any better, I would say industrial espionage."

"I have a tendency to agree with you. But, if I copied this item onto a CD or DVD, why not delete it and other files to confuse someone or to better cover my tracks? I mean, whoever did this knew that at some point we would discover what they had done."

"True, but I might, as the person who did this crime, be in some sort of a hurry. My report states that the CD or DVD was already labeled as 3RK126. This means that the CD or DVD was preformatted before coming into the facility."

"Okay, why, then, shoot my security officer?"

"Perhaps a matter of bad timing? You said yourself the other day that the wounds were non-life threatening."

"Yes, I did say that the security officer's injuries weren't life threatening in my official report to the Board of Directors. Joe is working the swing shift today, isn't he?"

"Yes."

"I'll meet him at the main gate and ask him if he turned off his computer that night or not."

"Okay."

Barry suddenly had an afterthought.

"Laura, are those computers in Lab 6 on a mainframe or do they have internal hard drives?"

"Both."

"Which means, anyone could have retrieved that information and put it onto a CD or DVD from any computer in either Lab 6 or the whole complex?"

"Yes. But, my people and I personally tracked it down to Lab 6, Joe Kapps' computer."

"Thank you, Laura, you can leave now."

Daniel walked into his office the next morning. He sat down at his desk when the phone rang. Lynn answered the phone and then called Daniel on the intercom.

"Daniel, Tom is on line 1," she said.

"Okay, got it," said Daniel, pressing the flashing light on his desktop phone.

"Tom, good to hear from you," said Daniel, smiling, even though he knew Tom couldn't see it through the phone.

"It's good to hear from you as well. The case for those two ladies is wrapping up nicely. I was able to get the charges dropped and their property returned to them. However, the assistant D.A. out here asked me a question that I don't have an answer for, so I thought I might call you for some help."

"What question did that nice assistant D.A. ask you?"

"On the lady who shot the boy who later died . . ."

"My sincere condolences to his family."

"I'll pass your condolences along. There is a mark on the lower, right side of her back that I can't explain. The mark looks like half a square with a horseshoe in the middle of it; what made that mark?"

"That's easy to explain, Tom."

"How so?"

"That mark came from the police officer's weapon. I'll bet she carries a Glock® in a small of the back holster that has what is called an FBI cant to it. That mark is from the back of the slide impacting the lower, right side area of her back."

"You're right on both statements, Daniel. The police report says the weapon was a Glock® Model 31. I'll let the assistant D.A. know.

"Are the police still holding the other boy?"

"Yes, until this thing wraps up."

"Have him charged with either the equivalency of first degree assault for choking my client out or have him charged federally."

"With what federal charges?"

"Do you have the rape kit test results back from the lab yet?" asked Daniel, thinking quickly to answer the question.

"Yes, I have them right here. What are you looking for, exactly?" asked Tom, almost afraid of the answer he was going to get in return.

"Did the lab test come back positive for either GHB or Ketamine®?"

"Yes, the lab did a gas spectrometry test on both the urine and blood samples submitted. Trace amounts of the post-cursors for GHB were detected."

"There's your answer. How about being an accessory before the fact, to the fact and after the fact. For possession of a Schedule I substance, dispensing a Schedule I substance without a DEA license number and distributing a Schedule I substance without a DEA license number."

"Okay, I'll pass those suggestions of yours along to the D.A. Boy, Daniel, you're really good."

"Thanks, Tom and bill me for your time if you want."

"Don't worry about it; this case was a tax write-off. Besides, I would have had to charge those ladies for fifteen hours of work at $605.00 an hour; goodbye."

"Goodbye."

Daniel put the phone down and went back to some of his pending cases. He had just come back from the Silverton Courthouse, when the office phone started ringing. Daniel picked up the phone only after he had checked the Caller ID® to see who it was; the answering service.

"This is Daniel."

"Mr. Marcos, I have a Mr. Berman on the line for you."

"Very well, put him through."

There was an audible click on the phone line.

"Mr. Marcos, I am being arrested by the FBI. They are taking me to Denver tonight," he said nervously, which Daniel picked up on right away.

"Calm down, Bill, what are the charges?" asked Daniel as he grabbed a legal pad and pen that were next to the phone.

"Willful Destruction of Government Property, Subsection L under Title 18, U.S.C as Amended."

"All right, put me on the phone with the FBI agent or agents."

"Yes, sir."

Bill handed the phone to the agent standing next to him on his right side.

"Hello?" said the agent.

"This is Attorney Daniel Marcos, Esquire. I will advise my client of his Constitutional rights. I am advising you and your partner DO NOT interrogate my client in any manner on the trip to Denver or prior to his arraignment."

"Okay, counselor."

"Furthermore, interrogation of my client without his attorney present during the trip will be considered a violation of at least two U.S. Supreme Court rulings on the matter from *Rhode Island V. Innis,* 1980, 446 U.S. 291 and *Nix V. Williams,* 1984, 467 U.S. 431. Any confession or evidence gained by the interrogation might be ruled inadmissible in Her Honor's court."

"I will abide by the rulings of the U.S. Supreme Court, counselor."

"Good, then hand the phone back over to my client."

"Yes, counselor."

The agent handed the phone back to Bill.

"Yes, Mr. Marcos?" asked Bill.

"As your duly appointed attorney, I am advising you of your Constitutional rights. You have the right to remain silent. Do not speak to anyone about this case without my presence or prior consent. Do not sign any documents they put in front of you, no matter what. You can only answer the following types of questions."

"Which are?" asked Bill as he grabbed a small pad of paper next to the phone and a pen.

"Your name, date of birth, Social Security number, age, height, weight, occupation, current address and any aliases that you have used in the past. You can answer questions about your shoe size, shirt size, pant size, marital status, but it just about ends there."

"Yes, sir, I wrote all of that down," said Bill.

"If you give up the right to remain silent, anything you say can and will be used against you in a court of law. Do you understand these rights as I have read them to you?"

"Yes."

"You have the right to an attorney and to have that attorney present with you at all stages of questioning. Do you understand these rights as I have read them to you?"

"Yes."

"If you cannot afford an attorney, the court will appoint you an attorney at no cost to you. Do you have and/or can you afford an attorney?"

"No, sir, I cannot afford an attorney."

"Well, you're in luck; your boss is paying my bill. You answered the question correctly for those listening ears on the other extension. Do you understand these rights as I have read them to you?"

"Yes, sir."

"Good answer, Bill. Having had your rights read to you, do you wish to make a statement to either myself or law enforcement representatives and do you have any questions about your rights as I have read them to you?"

"I do not wish to make a statement to anyone, until I have spoken with my attorney in private. I have no questions about my rights."

"Good answer, again, Bill. Enjoy your trip to Denver and I'll see you for the arraignment on Monday morning in Her Honor's court. Remember; do not talk to anyone about the case."

"I won't, sir; goodbye."

Daniel hung up the phone just as Lynn walked into the office.

"Lynn, call my clients for tomorrow afternoon. See if I can get continuances until next week sometime."

"Okay, what do I tell Linda at the D.A.'s office?"

"Tell her that I have a new client that is due to be arraigned Monday morning in Judge Johnson's courtroom and that I will be in Denver for a few days."

"Would that be Judge Krysta Johnson?"

"Yes. Now please hurry, the courts are going to close shortly."

Daniel went into his office and started packing up some things he thought he might need on his trip to Denver. He plugged his cell phone into its charging unit. He then started writing down some things on a legal pad he had on his desktop. By 1800 hours, Lynn had finished the final phone calls. She entered Daniel's office with her legal pad, which was filled with notes.

"Yes, Lynn?" asked Daniel as he looked up at her.

"Linda decided to drop the charges on cases 10CR19 and 10CR22."

"Good, call those clients and send them their final bills."

"Will do. Linda gave you until next Wednesday afternoon for cases 11CR26 and 12CR29."

"That's fair enough. I'm surprised she gave me that long."

"I thought so as well. Here's the writ of Habeas Corpus and the Discovery Motions," she said, handing Daniel the copies of the paperwork.

Daniel took the copies and put them on top of the stack of notes and other items that he then tossed into his briefcase. He closed the briefcase up and looked at Lynn.

"How did you know what paperwork I would want?"

"It seems fairly standard in all your cases that you take on. You want to see the prisoner and see the evidence being held against them."

"I see. Fax those forms to Krysta in the morning. After 1115 hours, I'll be on the road to Denver."

"Good luck."

"Thank you. One other thing, call Barry and tell him what's going on. Let him know that he needs to bring the retainer check to the office by next Friday, at the latest."

"Will do."

The next morning Daniel packed up several changes of clothes for his trip. He fueled up his car and parked it at the office. After the court case was disposed of at 1115 hours, Daniel checked his phone at the office for any messages. Since he didn't have any messages, he said goodbye to Lynn and drove to Denver. Daniel checked into a hotel not far from where his client was due in court on Monday morning. After a good night's sleep, Daniel drove out to the Federal Detention and Holding Facility in Lakewood, Colorado.

Daniel parked his car in one of the only parking spaces available. He emptied all of his pockets of anything metal. He left his cell phone in the car and only took a few pens and the car keys with him. He had a long walk up to the visitor's entrance. He pressed the button on the box that was to the left of the visitor's entrance gate. A voice came over the loudspeaker.

"State your name and business," said the voice.

"Attorney Daniel Marcos, Esquire. I'm here to see my client, Bill Berman."

"Proceed up the sidewalk to the window."

The gate lock buzzed a little bit as Daniel pulled it open. He shut the gate and proceeded up the sidewalk. He stopped at the window, which had a tray in the bottom of it like you would find at a bank teller window. He saw someone standing behind the window pointing to the telephone receiver to Daniel's right. Daniel picked up the phone.

"Place your driver's license, attorney credentials and all the objects in your pockets into the tray. Then step to your right and walk through the door."

Daniel emptied his pockets and stepped through the door. He was able to pick up all of his personal items except his driver's license. The security officer at the desk there kept it while issuing him a visitor's badge. Daniel clipped the badge to his upper left shirt pocket. The security officer then looked over the writ and handed it back to Daniel.

"Your client, sir, is in Attorney/Client room nine."

"Thank you."

Daniel entered the small room. Bill was dressed in an orange jump suit. He was handcuffed and Daniel could see leg irons were attached to his ankles. He was sitting in a chair. There was a small table and another chair for Daniel to sit down in. Daniel sat down in the chair and looked over at Bill.

"Bill, before you say anything, this place is probably equipped with video and audio recording devices. Be careful what you tell me," said Daniel, smiling.

"I understand, sir. Part of the USA PATRIOT ACT again, isn't it?"

"Yes. How was the trip?" asked Daniel.

"It was uneventful."

"Did the agents interrogate you?"

"No. All they asked me was if I had to go to the bathroom, what I wanted for lunch and how I wanted my coffee. I thought it was okay to answer the questions; right?"

"Of course, how are the accommodations?"

"Great, if you ask me. I'm on the east wing with only two other inmates."

"Good. Do you want a soda, a cup of coffee or a snack?"

"No, thank you, sir."

"I'm only going to ask you one question right now. Did you notice anything or anyone unusual the night you were shot?"

"Yeah, I ran into Bob Quinest that night. Normally, he and I have a good conversation that keeps me thinking and awake all night long; not that night though."

"What happened?" asked Daniel as he started taking mental notes for later transcription.

"I said hello to him and he simply marched past me with an angry look on his face. It wasn't until I checked my email that night, I found out he had been terminated."

"Where did he live up to that point?"

"Silverton."

"Does he still live there?"

"I don't know. If he does still live there, he lives in apartment 12A on a street that begins with the letter B."

"Okay. Now, I can't tell you everything I suspect, but someone or some entity wants you out of the way. Now, I want you to think about my statement to you and try and get some rest. I'll see you in court on Monday morning."

"Okay."

The guards came and opened up the back door to the room as Daniel was leaving through the front door. He drove back to his hotel and went directly to his hotel room. Daniel called the answering service and left a message to have Lynn call him on his cell phone right away. Lynn called Daniel on his cell phone a few minutes later.

"Daniel, good to hear from you. How is our client doing?" she asked.

"Fine. Look, call Jessica and have her drive around Silverton. Have her find all the streets that begin with the letter B and when she finds those streets, see how many of them have apartments on them. I'm looking for an apartment 12A and the occupant should be one Bob Quinest."

"Got it, what else?" she asked, because she knew Daniel had more on his mind.

"Call Barry and tell him I need to talk to him. Tell Barry to call me on my cell phone."

"Right away."

"Goodbye."

Two hours later, Barry finally called Daniel back.

"Daniel, what can I do for you?" asked Barry.

"A lot. First off, on the night Bill was shot, did HR terminate an employee, with or without cause, by the name of Bob Quinest?"

"Yes, I believe that I have the email; why?"

"Barry, I highly suspect, although I cannot prove it right now, that Bill was shot by Bob for only one of two reasons that I can think of. One, Bill knew or stumbled onto something illegal that involved Bob. Two, Bill was in the wrong place at the wrong time."

"Funny you should mention the first possibility. The CIO mentioned something about industrial espionage to me a few days ago."

"Barry, I'll be back on Thursday morning. Be at my office first thing in the morning with a list of projects that Bob was working on at the time of his termination."

"Should this listing include the projects that he had, or could have had, access to?"

"Yes, can you arrange an after-hours tour of the facility for my private investigator?"

"Sure, will she be taking pictures or anything like that?"

"Yes, she will be taking lots of pictures and possibly running some tests. A lot has to do with what happens in court on Monday morning."

"Okay, I'll get her cleared for a vendor's pass for Lab 6. Does she have a clean criminal history?"

"Yes, I'll contact you after court."

"I'll be waiting."

Daniel hung up his cell phone and went to bed after taking a shower.

CHAPTER 5

Barry decided to come in on a Sunday morning. When he arrived at work, the CIO was already there. Barry went to his office, did some paperwork and walked around with Harry, the weekend, day shift security officer. When Barry had returned to his office, the CIO was waiting outside for him. She had a stack of computer printouts. They walked inside Barry's office and shut the door. Barry pushed in the button lock inside of the door handle for privacy reasons. He sat down and stared at the CIO.

"What did you and your specialty teams find out, Laura?" asked Barry as he looked at the stack of computer printouts and started going through them.

"Several things, but none of them make any sense," she replied.

"What's the first thing you found?"

"Bob was in charge, in Lab 6, of a file folder called DARPA on the mainframe. The file folder is huge, filling up about 500 gigabytes of information with some 254 subfolders. The main file folder contains both pictures and text files. I must be a little dense, but what does DARPA stand for?"

"DARPA stands for Defense Advanced Research Projects Agency. It would appear that Bob had access to a lot of interesting things. What projects did he have access to and what projects was he directly in charge of?" he asked, still going through the printouts.

"Well, that's the second thing that doesn't make any sense. I looked over the files and they fall into one of two of the most unusual categories."

"Which are?"

"A Directed Energy Systems subfolder and a Counter Weapons Systems subfolder."

"Bob did have at least a SECRET clearance and he had worked for two other major defense contractors which were Boeing and Raytheon. Neither one reported any disciplinary problems with him."

"Then this other thing I found out won't make any sense either. The file he copied was his own invention. DARPA didn't want it according to their reject letter."

"A reject letter could make someone a little angry and bitter; what else did you find?"

"Inside of the Counter Weapons Systems subfolder, there was another invention of his. He called it an SSLMD."

"What does SSLMD stand for, anyway?"

"I think it stands for Sub Surface Launched Missile Decoy."

"What was DARPA's stand on that idea of his?"

"They wanted it very badly. They negotiated a deal with Bob through a third party by the name of Paul Hockadae. Paul paid Bob an undisclosed amount of money for the idea."

"That's interesting, now I know why Bob was fired. Taking any monetary compensation for an idea that was done on company time or equipment is grounds for dismissal."

"Who is this Paul Hockadae? His name sounds familiar to me for some reason," said Laura.

"Paul Hockadae is one of, or at least he used to be one of, Boeing's top military contracts personnel. He also used to work for Raytheon in Research and Development of weapons systems."

"Like I said, nothing of what I found makes any sense."

"Good job, Laura. I will see you tomorrow morning at the weekly meeting," Barry replied, totally evading the earlier statement. He unlocked the door and they both went home. Barry made one phone call before going to bed.

The next morning, Daniel arrived at the federal courthouse early. He went through the security checkpoint and proceeded to courtroom 10. When he arrived, the prosecutor was preparing his opening statements and arranging the evidence on the table that was in the center of the courtroom.

Daniel sat down to his right side, instead of the usual left side, as Daniel was used to in other courtrooms. Bill was already there as Daniel sat down in one of three chairs at the table marked DEFENDANT. Daniel had just opened up his briefcase, when the prosecutor dropped copies of the reports, statements and evidence for the case into Daniel's briefcase.

"I know that you have already submitted the Discovery Motions paperwork, but as of yet, I have not formally received them. I was told that for a criminal defense attorney, you are very thorough," he said.

"Thank you," replied Daniel as he started going over the paperwork.

"Good morning, Mr. Marcos," said Bill.

"Good morning, Bill. Did they feed you before you were brought to court?" asked Daniel.

"Yes, they fed me."

"How are your bullet wounds doing?"

"Fine. The detention center doctor has examined them several times. The nurses make sure that I get my antibiotics and painkillers on time, while I am up here."

"That's good news. I would hate to think that they would take a chance on violating your 8th Amendment right against cruel or unusual punishment."

The door to the left side of the courtroom opened. The bailiff stood up to address the court.

"All rise, the arraignment hearing in the case of *The U.S. Government v. Bill Berman,* case number 14CR1111 is now in session. The Honorable Judge Krysta Johnson, presiding."

She walked up the three steps to her bench. She opened up the case file and banged her gavel down.

"You may be seated."

Everyone sat down as she scanned over the complete case file. She kept it open as she looked down at both the prosecution's table and the defendant's table. She saw Daniel sitting there at the Defendant's table and smiled at him.

"Is the prosecution ready with formal charges against the defendant?" she asked.

"Yes, Your Honor, I am ready," replied the man.

"Where's your assistant prosecution counsel?" she asked.

"I'm on my own on this one, Your Honor," he replied as he fumbled with some paperwork and the case file.

"Very well. Daniel, good to see you in my courtroom," she said.

"Good to see you as well, Your Honor."

"Prosecution, please read into the court record the charges against the defendant."

"Your Honor, may I address the court?" asked Daniel.

"Does the prosecution have any objections to defense counsel's request?"

"None, Your Honor."

"Very well, proceed Mr. Marcos."

"Thank you, Your Honor. I have advised my client of his Constitutional rights and the charges that the government has leveled against him. Furthermore, my client waives the reading of the charges and requests to go straight to the preliminary hearing," said Daniel.

"Any particular reason for this request, counselor?"

"Yes, Your Honor. I have two other cases pending back in Silverton and my friend and yours, Linda Bacara, only granted me an extension until this Wednesday."

“I see. Is the prosecution ready with its case and evidence?”

“Yes, Your Honor and I have given defense counsel copies of everything in the case file.”

“Very well, allow me to consult my appointment calendar,” replied Krysta as she pulled out her appointment calendar from under her microphone at the bench.

“Take your time, Your Honor,” said Daniel as he went back to reading the reports in the case file.

“I have tomorrow afternoon at 1400 hours available; is that soon enough?” asked Krysta.

“I’ll see you tomorrow afternoon, Your Honor. I would like to confer with my client in private at this time,” said Daniel.

“Okay. Marshal Smith, would you please escort Mr. Marcos and his client to the attorney/client room at the end of the hallway?”

“Yes, Your Honor. This way please,” said Marshal Smith, using his left hand to point down the left hallway.

“Very well, bailiff, next case please.”

Daniel packed up all of his stuff and followed the Marshal to the room that was at the end of the hallway. Bill sat down in one of the ten chairs in the room. There was a large, wooden table in the center of the room. Daniel waited until the Marshal had closed the door and Daniel heard the latch click into place before speaking.

“I’ve read over most of the statements, reports and photocopies of the evidence gathered. Someone has gone to great lengths to get you into enough trouble to keep you out of the picture for a while. Now, I have some questions for you,” said Daniel as he opened up his briefcase, pulling out a legal pad and pen.

“Go ahead, ask me any questions you want,” replied Bill.

“Tell me about your duty weapon,” said Daniel.

“It is a Glock® Model 20, firing the 10mm-automatic round with night sights and several 17-round magazines.”

“What type of duty ammunition are you issued by Barry?”

“Federal manufactures the ammunition. It is a 180-grain, Hydrashock® round.”

"So, Barry doesn't issue you CCI Blazer® rounds for duty use?"

"No. Those rounds are only used for target practice and our requalifications every three months."

"Do you personally own any other firearms, specifically handguns, which fire a 10-mm automatic round?"

"Yes. It is a Colt® Delta Elite, but it's in the shop in Durango for repairs."

"Do you happen to know the name of the shop, a phone number, etc.?"

"Yes. The place is called The Four Corners Rod and Gun Shop. The gunsmith's name is Lou."

"You know that I will check your story out, right?"

"Yes, sir. In fact, I fully expected it and if you didn't do it, I would have been really surprised."

"Do you remember the serial number of your weapon?"

"Yes, it's CDE8644."

"I'll check on that, as well. Where do you and your fellow security officers shoot and qualify?"

"At the facility in Lab 5. Lab 5 can handle handguns, rifles, shotguns and machineguns of all calibers."

"Can anyone use Lab 5 as an employee of the facility?"

"Yes. It requires a special access code from Barry after you have registered the weapon or weapons with him and the armory guy that's in a wheelchair."

"That's good information to know. I'll have to make some phone calls. How many rounds do you think you fired at the perpetrator that night?"

"At least six, maybe more. I think the last two rounds went into the elevator doors as they were closing."

"So, you don't think you hit your target?"

"No, I was moving, they were moving and obviously neither of us hit each other fatally. My wounds were non-life threatening."

"Do you own the .25-caliber semi-automatic handgun they have in evidence?"

"Yes, it's a family heirloom of sorts. My grandfather bought it for my grandmother. My grandmother gave it to my mother who, when I was born, gave it to me when I was legally able to possess such a thing."

"Is it a Smith and Wesson?" asked Daniel, remembering from the ballistics report that it was a Beretta.

"No, it's a Beretta."

"The ballistics report states they couldn't match up the shells they test fired to the shells provided. Did you mark up the inside of the barrel with a metal object of some kind to throw off the ballistics test?"

"No."

"Do you remember the last time you fired the weapon?"

"I think it was four months ago."

"Good, I will be making a lot of phone calls tonight to verify some of this information that you have given me. For tonight, I want you to think long and hard about this question."

"Which is?"

"At anytime, prior to this incident, did you have any trouble with any employee at the facility no matter how small a problem?"

Daniel stood up from the table and put everything back into his briefcase. He opened the door and the Marshal took Bill away to a waiting van. Daniel went back to his hotel and had lunch. As he sat down at the desk that was in the hotel room, his cell phone started ringing. He looked at the number on the screen; it was Jessica.

"Yes Jessica, what did you find out?"

"Bob Quinest lives on Birch Street, Apartment 12A in Silverton."

"Did you make contact with him?"

"No, he wasn't home so I left one of my business cards in the front door frame."

"Did you date and time stamp your card?"

"I sure did, Daniel, because I knew you would ask me that question."

"Good girl. Now, I need you to personally call on a person by the name of Lou at a place called the Four Corners Rod and Gun Shop in Durango. I need to know if Bill dropped off his Colt® Delta Elite, 10-mm Automatic pistol to Lou a few days ago."

"Okay, I'll call you back later then; goodbye."

"Goodbye."

Daniel called Lynn and told her to have Barry call Daniel back on Daniel's cell phone. Lynn called Barry, who called Daniel back right away.

"Yes, Daniel what can I do for you?"

"Do you have a record of any kind of the calibers of weapons that go into and out of Lab 5?"

"Yes, I have a complete log. Why don't you tell me what you're looking for and maybe I can find it for you?"

"How many people shoot weapons there, specifically, handguns that fire the 10mm Automatic round?"

"Hold on," said Barry as he began typing in the information into the computer. The computer told him the answer was 30.

"30, Daniel."

"Eliminate security personnel."

"Okay," said Barry as he narrowed the search parameters. The computer told him the list had been narrowed down to 23.

"23, Daniel. Incidentally, both Bob Quinest's name and Bill Berman's name came up on that list."

"What does Bob allegedly shoot?"

"The Smith and Wesson Models 610 and 1006."

"Thank you, Barry. You've just put together a large piece of the puzzle. I'll talk to you later."

"Goodbye," said Barry as he hung up his phone.

Daniel had just set his cell phone down when Jessica called him.

"Yes, Jessica, what did you find out? I thought I told you to go see the gunsmith personally?"

"The gunsmith confirmed all the information you gave me to confirm. He even told me what was wrong with the firearm. He further told me that he heard about this case in the news and was happy to cooperate with me when I told him who I was gathering the information for."

"What is wrong with my client's firearm?"

"A broken firing pin."

"That means the firearm is inoperable; thank you. When I get back on Wednesday, let's pay a social call on Mr. Quinest together."

"Fine by me, goodbye."

"Goodbye."

Daniel hung up the phone and had dinner. After dinner, he walked around the area surrounding the hotel. He returned to his hotel room after dark, took a shower and went to sleep. The alarm on his cell phone started going off so that he could get breakfast after working out in the hotel gym. After breakfast, he wrote down some more notes and took a nap. He left his hotel room and had lunch on the way to the courthouse. When he arrived in the courtroom, Bill was already there waiting for Daniel at the Defendant's table.

"Good afternoon, Daniel," he said.

"Good afternoon. Do you have an answer for me?" asked Daniel as he opened up his briefcase and prepared to take notes.

"Yes, I had to write up an informational incident report on four separate occasions concerning two visitors that had come to see Bob after-hours. Without prior clearance from Barry, no visitors are allowed into the facility after 1800 hours and at no time on the weekends or holidays."

"Good corporate policy. Would you recognize these men again if you saw them?"

"Absolutely, but as far as exact dates, I don't remember."

"That's okay. Do you remember a date range?"

"Last year in February, June and October."

"I'll call your boss and find out for sure."

As Judge Johnson walked into her courtroom and everyone went through the motions of rising for the judge, Barry's phone started ringing. He had just finished off sending a dozen or so emails as he reached over to grab the receiver.

"Hello?" asked Barry.

"Barry, it's Paul Hockadae, you called me yesterday. How long has it been since we last spoke to each other?"

"About eight years now, I think. Since that last security symposium in Colorado Springs, Colorado."

"What can I do for you?"

"Answer the question that I am about to ask you and don't lie to me."

"Okay, go ahead."

"Did you buy anything from Bob Quinest recently?"

"Yes. He sent me a copy of the idea he said he had come up with and our research and development personnel sent him a check for $125,565.00."

"Was that idea he sent you called an SSLMD, by any chance?"

"Yes and funny you should be asking me about that idea because the U.S. Patents and Trademarks Office just sent me the patent number for the idea."

"What is the patent number?"

"8,777,777. Is there anything else I can do for you, Barry?"

"No, you answered all of my questions. Thank you for calling me back."

"Anytime, Barry, anytime; goodbye."

Barry knew as he hung up the phone, that for the next Monday morning Board of Directors meeting, some hard questions would have to be asked. It looked more and more like what the CIO had thought she said it was; industrial espionage. Barry only hoped that Daniel was doing better.

CHAPTER 6

Daniel was waiting for the prosecutor, Gary, to finish off his opening statements to the court. When Gary finished, Daniel sat at the table for a few minutes trying to gather his thoughts. Krysta looked down at Daniel before speaking.

"Is defense counsel ready with their opening statements to this court?" asked Krysta.

Daniel stood up, cleared his throat and nodded his head up and down.

"Boy, after those opening statements by my esteemed colleague, I guess I have a guilty client. But you know, Your Honor, I don't have guilty clients and even if I did have one, I would still vehemently defend their Constitutional rights to the end from an overzealous Executive branch. Besides, Your Honor, you are also keenly aware that I am a very thorough defense attorney," said Daniel, who was just warming up.

"Yes, indeed counselor, I am aware of such things," she replied as she nodded her head up and down in agreement.

"Your Honor, my client pleads not guilty to the charge of Willful Destruction of Government Property by Use of a Firearm. My client invokes his affirmative defense privilege in using deadly force against someone else who was using deadly force against my client. Simply put, self-defense."

Daniel turned towards the prosecutor before continuing with his opening statements.

"My client, Your Honor, is authorized to use all levels of force up to deadly force in Lab 6 by the government's own admission. There is a sign saying such at the entrance to the lab. This gives my client another affirmative defense to the charge."

"Objection, Your Honor. The government has many such signs at all sorts of installations all over the globe. It is nothing more than a scare tactic meant to keep out people who value their life."

"Your Honor, scare tactic or not, I don't believe a sign would be posted at any installation if there wasn't something within the area of the sign that the government didn't want to get out of that area. It is only common sense," said Daniel.

"Objection overruled, continue counselor," replied Krysta.

"Mr. Prosecutor's allegations of a conspiracy theory, as he stated in his opening statements, I don't buy for a minute, Your Honor. If such a conspiracy existed, then Mr. Prosecutor here would have to prove that, on the night of the shootout, my client and the gun sat down at the kitchen table or wherever and planned it so that the gun would arrive at the facility after my client was on duty. The gun would then have to sneak its way down to Lab 6 and set off the alarms. Then the gun would have to be waiting to ambush my client when he came to check out the alarms."

"Objection, Your Honor, defense counsel is trying to confuse this court!" said Gary, rather loudly.

"Objection noted and overruled. Mr. Prosecutor, you did say words to that effect in your opening statements to this court; continue counselor."

"Thank you, Your Honor. We are here in this courtroom because my client did his job. The property damage that was caused was a direct result of several factors that were beyond my client's control."

"Like what factors, Mr. Marcos?" asked Gary, venomously.

"My client, upon surprising the individual, was involved in a gunfight. The individual, whom I shall from now on refer to as the perpetrator, began moving and shooting at my client. My client, moved out of the way of the incoming fire, just like his training had taught him to do in a case like that, and returned fire. My client thankfully, sustained only minor, non-life threatening injuries. During this mêlée, my client's bulletproof vest and radio were destroyed. If anything, my client should be able to get restitution from the perpetrator, if they are ever caught, for the replacement costs of the bulletproof vest and the radio."

Daniel waited before continuing. Daniel could see the look of confusion on Mr. Gary's face.

"My client is an armed security officer, Your Honor, and is not held to the same high degree of training and firearms marksmanship standards as, say, an FBI agent or a U.S. Marshal. My client and the perpetrator were shooting at each other at a distance, my client estimated to be, about 30-yards/10-meters, in the dark. As far as my client attempting to destroy evidence in his own case, my client could not have done such an act."

"Why not, he had plenty of time," said Gary, sarcastically.

"No, he did not, Mr. Prosecutor. Your Honor, please look at the prosecution's exhibits L and M. L is the discharge paperwork for my client from the Telluride Trauma Center that had treated him for his gunshot wounds. If you look at the time of discharge, it was date and time stamped in the lower left corner at 0548 hours. It is a known fact that no one but the patient can receive the discharge paperwork to leave a treatment facility with the exception of invalids and juveniles."

"So what, counselor, your client still had plenty of time. It's only a ten minute drive for your client to get to his apartment and destroy the evidence."

"Obviously, Your Honor, this was evidence that an anonymous tipster, in this case I will say it was the same person who shot my client, alleged that Bill was going to destroy. The tipster didn't bother to check out where Bill had been treated for his wounds, therefore, the tipster wrongly assumed, in this case, that Bill had been treated in Silverton."

"I thought you would start crying about the no search warrant for the evidence that was gathered," said Gary, flatly.

"I have no problem with the evidence that was gathered. The tip would have indicated to the FBI agents exigent circumstances existed; no time to obtain a proper search warrant and fully protected by the U.S. Supreme Court on more than one occasion and even state supreme courts have protected exigent circumstances. Besides, the evidence gathered is exculpatory to my client."

"Exculpatory to your client? How so, Mr. Marcos?" asked Gary, now a little more aware of his own short-sightedness.

"The shell casings that were seized are the wrong type for my client's duty and personal weapons. The only things that match on those shell casings are the calibers and I must let the court know that my client's personal firearm has a broken firing pin in it, therefore, it is inoperable and could not have been used to commit any shooting of any kind until it is repaired."

"Objection, Your Honor, defense counsel is trying to mislead this court again with another red herring scheme."

"Objection overruled. Defense counsel has yet to fail to prove that any evidence is inculpatory to his client," said Krysta in return to the outburst in her courtroom.

"Thank you again, Your Honor. Prosecution's exhibit M is the report filed by the lead FBI agent assigned to the case. The agent states in his report that he and his partner arrived at or about 0630 hours, to my client's apartment, to begin the search. It is a known fact that the distance from Telluride to Silverton requires at least 120 minutes to drive."

"You know that for a fact, counselor?" asked Gary, suspicious as to the validity of the statement.

"Yes, I do. I have driven that route several times in the past twelve months. If you doubt me on the time or distance, then may I suggest you consult MapQuest®."

"I will check on that statement, Your Honor, if you don't mind, counselor," said Gary as he handed the information to his legal assistant who left the courtroom.

"Does defense counsel have anything else to say?" asked Krysta.

"The trip, Your Honor, would mean that my client, at the very earliest, could not have arrived back to his apartment in Silverton before 0755 hours. I was asked by my client's boss, Mr. Barry Goldman, to stop by my client's place to check on him. His boss seemed genuinely concerned about my client's welfare."

"Do you know what time you allegedly arrived?" asked Gary.

"It was approximately 0800 hours. My client stated to me, at that time, that he had just arrived home only a few minutes earlier to find the FBI agents gathering evidence. Calling your attention to prosecution exhibit D, the ballistics report, shows inconsistencies."

"The evidence gathered were the 10mm Automatic shells that the tipster said we would find along with the .25-caliber semi-automatic weapon," said Gary.

"Yes, evidence which the tipster alleged that my client used to self-inflict his own wounds. If you read paragraph nine of the report on page four, you will find that the weapon submitted for testing did not match the bullets removed from my client."

"So, your client could have scratched up the barrel rifling with a scribe or other similar metal instrument."

"Not likely, Mr. Prosecutor. My client stated to me that the weapon taken was a family heirloom of sorts. Why would he want to damage an heirloom?"

"I don't know. What about the 10mm Automatic shells we found?"

"Placed there to make you take the tipster's bait. The tipster meant for you to chase your tail around in circles on dead-end leads."

"So, what you're saying is, we've been duped in some manner?"

"Yes. The tipster needed to buy himself or herself some time to get away. They carefully planned this little action to frame my client."

"Your client owns a 10-mm Automatic. Did you know that, counselor?"

"Yes, I was aware of such a matter. My client, in fact, owns a Colt® Delta Elite 10mm Automatic pistol which is currently in a repair shop in Durango, as I stated earlier."

"It is?" said Gary, a little surprised by the information once again.

"Yes, I independently verified my client's claim yesterday afternoon. The ballistics technician also states in paragraph three on page one that the weapon submitted for testing, 'had dust accumulation on certain internal parts when I disassembled the weapon. This indicates a stored condition of a minimum of 90-days.'"

"So what, remember we did find shell casings for both weapons."

"I would like to point out to you, Mr. Prosecutor, that those shell casings, according to paragraph eleven, page five, states that the shell casings were CCI-Blazer® rounds. My client's duty issue ammunition is from Federal, not CCI."

"What does that prove?" asked Gary, looking more confused.

"I propose, Your Honor, that if a detailed inspection of those shell casings is done by the ballistics technician, I believe you will find, Mr. Prosecutor and Your Honor, that those shell casings came from either a Smith and Wesson Model 610 revolver or a Smith and Wesson Model 1006 semi-automatic pistol and not a Glock®. The other shell casings were CCI-Blazer® rounds. The Winchester® rounds that were removed from my client at the trauma center, have yet to be ballistically matched to my client's weapon."

"Just how would you know what gun fires what rounds, etc., defense counsel?" asked Krysta.

"Simple, Your Honor. If a shell is ejected out of a semi-automatic or fully automatic weapon, there will be two, manufacturer's distinct, marks from the extractor and the ejector. Also, the firing pin impact mark on the primer is unique. Glock® has a rectangular shaped firing pin impact mark."

"Mr. Prosecutor, have the ballistics technician do an inspection on those shell casings. We will be in recess until the results are available."

"Yes, Your Honor," said Gary as he left the room with the evidence from the evidence table.

An hour and half later, the results were ready. The court reconvened and the FBI ballistics technician addressed the court.

"Your Honor, I have completed the inspection on those spent shell casings per the prosecution's orders. For defense counsel's records, I have been a ballistics technician with the FBI for over ten years," she said.

"That's a most impressive resumé, however this court wants to know the answer to the questions that were raised by defense counsel," said Krysta.

"In my expert opinion and after a careful inspection of the shell casings, they did not come from a semi-automatic or fully automatic weapon of the same caliber. Furthermore, the firing pin impact mark does not match that of a Glock®. The firing pin impact mark appears very consistent with a Smith and Wesson Model 610 revolver and not a Smith and Wesson Model 1006," she said confidently.

"Thank you very much, madam. In light of this new development that has been brought out in open court, Your Honor, I move for a dismissal of the charges against my client. I further request that when the perpetrator is found, my colleague can prosecute them fully and I will lend all assistance to the prosecution that they may need," said Daniel.

"Prosecution, do you have any objections to a dismissal of the charges?" asked Krysta.

"No, the government concurs on the dismissal of the charges against the defendant."

"The charges are hereby dismissed. The defendant is free to go and will get back all personal property seized by the government," said Krysta, banging her gavel down.

"Thank you, Mr. Marcos," said Bill as the Marshal prepared to lead Bill away.

"Thank you, Bill. Marshal, when will my client be ready to go home?"

"It takes up to 24 hours for all of the paperwork to clear. He can go home tomorrow morning, Mr. Marcos," replied the Marshal.

"Thank you, Marshal. May I have some private time to confer with my client?"

"Sure, I'll go stand over there in the right corner of the courtroom. Just wave when you're done. By the way, you're a most impressive attorney in court. I now know why some prosecutors up here fear you," said the Marshal as he walked over to the corner.

"Bill, I've seen some pretty good frame up jobs in my time, but this one was well thought out from beginning to end. Somebody went through the trouble of going through thousands of spent rounds of ammunition in Lab 5 looking for a particular caliber. They even went so far as to use a pay phone in Glenwood Springs to cover their tracks."

"Thank you, Mr. Marcos, for telling me all of this. I gather that you want me to keep up my guard then?"

"Yes and you're welcome. Something tells me when the tipster finds out that you're free, they're going to come after you again, only this time it will be different. Keep your Colt® handy."

"Will do."

"Do you have transportation back to Silverton?"

"No."

"I'll send my private investigator to pick you up. Unless something else comes up, my time is done with you," said Daniel, waving his left hand. The Marshal came over.

"Marshal, my private investigator will be coming up here to pick up my client, is that okay?"

"Yes, sir. Just tell me their name and I will pass it along to the out service processors."

"Her name is Jessica Kim, she's an Asian female and drives a black, 2008 model year Jeep® Grand Cherokee, 4-door."

"Okay."

Daniel packed up his briefcase and went back to his hotel room. He packed up all of his stuff and walked down to his car. He put all of his clothes into the backseat and checked out of the hotel. When he arrived back at his car, he looked at his cell phone. Lynn had called him a couple of times. He stepped into his car, put on his seatbelt and called Lynn.

"Hello Daniel, how did court go?" she asked.

"Very well, I think. Mr. Berman is a free man for now. What is Jessica doing right now?"

"I think she's still doing nighttime surveillance on the Hawthorne property to see who's been stealing his cows and sheep."

"Personally, I think Mr. Hawthorne is going crazy. I seriously doubt anyone is stealing those animals. I think it's more likely bobcats, lynxes, mountain lions or bears that are taking the animals. Or it might be aliens stealing them for experiments."

"Yeah, you're probably right about that," she said, laughing a little.

"Call Jessica and ask her to come up to Denver tonight and pick up my client, Mr. Berman. He's scheduled to be released tomorrow morning around 0800 hours."

"Who's going to do her surveillance then?"

"I'll do that for tonight for a few hours. Tell Jessica to be very careful on the trip up to and back from Denver. Make sure that Barry is billed for mileage and time for both myself and Jessica."

"Okay, I'll start making phone calls; goodbye."

Daniel turned onto Southbound I-25. He stopped in Walsenburg to get something to eat. He refueled his car in Alamosa and finally arrived in Silverton just before nightfall. Daniel changed clothes after taking a shower. He put all of his dirty clothes into the laundry room.

He grabbed his Glock® Model 20 with night sights on it along with the holster and four of the ten special made, 25-round magazines. He strapped three of the extra magazines to his left thigh and put the fourth one into the gun.

He drove out to the Hawthorne property and parked where Jessica normally parked. He turned on the monitor that he had in his car, which was tuned into the sensors that Jessica had placed in the valley in front of him to keep an eye on the cows and sheep. He turned the volume up all the way on the monitor so that he could hear anything that came close to the animals.

Daniel could hear the cows and sheep that were in the valley in front of him. Sometime about 0100 hours, he accidentally dozed off. He was awakened by something going past his car. He woke up, looked around and, not seeing anything, went back to sleep.

A truck had driven past him. The truck had a small crate that was built into the bed of the truck and it was dragging some chains behind it to cover the tire tracks. The driver had turned off the headlights when he had turned off the main road onto the county road that led into the valley. The three occupants were grinning at each other because they thought they had slipped past whoever it was in the car they had passed. When the driver applied the brakes, the brakes squealed. That squeal woke Daniel up immediately making him grab his pistol to look around the area.

Daniel looked out his windshield to see lights in the valley in front of him. He quickly pushed the RECORD button on the side of the monitor so that the flash drive could record everything that was going on. Daniel was going to give the flash drive to law enforcement personnel when they arrived to arrest the persons in the vehicle. Daniel grabbed his cell phone and called the San Juan County Sheriff's Department's non-emergency number. Daniel was told to wait where he was at and that a deputy was on the way.

A few minutes later, Deputy Gilda Hold showed up. She parked her car in front of Daniel's and walked over to where Daniel was standing. She could see one of the 25-round magazines sticking out of Daniel's gun. She then saw the other three that were strapped to his left thigh. She approached with some caution with her left hand on her service weapon and the retaining strap unsnapped.

"Damn, counselor, were you planning on starting a war with these people tonight?" she asked, pointing at all the magazines and ammunition.

"I wasn't sure how long it would take to get help," replied Daniel, smiling.

"Okay, counselor. How many of them do you think there are?"

"I could hear three distinct voices and they were all talking in Spanish. Something tells me you're going to find out-of-country license plates on their vehicle and you're probably going to find phony paperwork for transporting animals across both statelines and U.S. Borders."

"Okay, I'll call for another deputy who can speak Spanish. What evidence do you have to support your theory?" she asked as she started her report.

"All the evidence I believe you will need is on this flash drive here and you can keep the flash drive," replied Daniel handing the deputy the flash drive.

"Thank you, counselor. You can go home now."

"Thanks and my client will be willing to press charges against these people," said Daniel as he started up his car, turned off the monitor and drove home.

Daniel arrived at his house in Silverton around 0230 hours. He went to bed and woke up to his alarm clock going off in his right ear. Daniel stretched before working out and went to court. Linda dismissed both cases because the first case had lack of hard evidence and in the second case, the victim refused to press charges.

Daniel returned to his office, had a cup of coffee and started going over his notes he had made up in Denver during the preliminary hearing. After he had reviewed the notes, he gave them to Lynn to type up and put into Bill Berman's case file. A little past 1500 hours, Jessica walked into the office to drop off the mileage sheets to Lynn. Daniel came out and put down his cup of coffee. Jessica looked up and smiled.

"How was the trip?" asked Daniel.

"Unusual. More than once, I had to lose what I think were two 'tails.'"

"Good work, girl. How about we pay a social call on Mr. Bob Quinest?"

Jessica and Daniel drove to Bob's place. They walked up the stairs to his apartment. As Daniel knocked on the doorframe a few times, he saw the pile of newspapers on the doorstep. Daniel saw Jessica's business card still stuck in the doorframe. He pulled out a pen from his inside, right jacket pocket and tried to push open the mail slot.

The slot was completely blocked by mail. He put the pen back into the pocket it had come out of after he had written on the back of his own business card. He stuck his business card into the doorframe below Jessica's.

Jessica was using her small flashlight to look inside the window to the right of the front door, when a large blowfly landed on the inside of the window; Jessica jumped back a little bit.

"Something wrong, Jessica?" asked Daniel.

"It was just that I was looking in the windows to see if I could see Bob and this big blowfly landed on the inside of the window; kind of scared me," she said pointing at the window.

It is too early in the year for flies of any kind at this altitude, thought Daniel to himself.

Daniel looked back down at the pile of newspapers and then back at the blocked mail slot. He pulled out his cell phone from the front left pocket of his suit jacket and called the Silverton Town Marshal's office. Marshal Nancy Gills answered.

"Thank you for calling the Silverton Town Marshal's office, Marshal Gills speaking, how can I help you?" she said.

"Marshal Gills, this is Attorney Daniel Marcos, listen to me closely," he started saying but was interrupted by Nancy.

"Well counselor, did you find another corpse?" she said, almost laughing at Daniel. She read the article in the newspaper about Daniel finding a corpse in one of his other cases.

"Why yes, I think I did find a corpse. How did you know?" asked Daniel, having been caught a little off guard by her remark.

"Oh, just a lucky guess. Why don't you tell me what you found, counselor," she replied as she started taking notes for a possible report later.

"My private investigator and I were paying a social call on the alleged occupant of apartment 12A here on Birch Street. We found at least a week and half's worth of newspapers and the mail slot is completely blocked by mail. Also, there is a large blowfly on the inside of the window to the right of the front door. It is much too early in the year at this altitude for flies of any kind."

"Okay, I'll come over and do a welfare check on the apartment's occupant or occupants."

"That's fine, but I seriously suggest you bring along the Silverton Medical Examiner and the San Juan County Coroner."

"Okay counselor, we'll be right over in a few minutes. Don't go anywhere until I've had a chance to get statements from both you and your private investigator."

"We'll be waiting."

CHAPTER 7

Daniel and Jessica were sitting on the front steps leading up to the apartment when the Silverton Medical Examiner arrived. He parked his car by the house that was next to the small apartment building, stepped out of his car and closed the door. On the driver and passenger side doors, was the State of Colorado Seal. On the outside of the seal it read "Town of Silverton Medical Examiner Bob Boyington." Bob walked up the stairs towards Daniel.

"Hello, counselor, good to see you," he said as he shook Daniel's right hand.

"Good to see you, Bob," replied Daniel.

"Jessica, how are you, madam?" he asked as he shook her left hand.

"Fine."

"Daniel, I really hope, for your sake, we do find a body or bodies in there. Otherwise, I think the coroner will have you arrested."

Everyone started laughing. A few minutes later, the Silverton Town Marshal arrived. She stepped out of her vehicle as Nabiya Quartez, the San Juan County Coroner, arrived. Nabiya slammed on her brakes and parked just behind Bob's car. She stepped out of her official coroner vehicle and marched right up to Nancy.

"I was eating my dinner, Nancy, when you called me. If we don't find a corpse or corpses in this apartment, I want him arrested for false reporting to authorities!" yelled Nabiya, while pointing her left index finger at Daniel.

"If this turns out to be a false alarm, which I doubt it is, then I will gladly be arrested by Nancy here. She can charge me with violating Colorado Revised Statutes 18-8-111, False Reporting to Authorities. Besides, it would give Linda a great amount of pleasure to prosecute me, Marshal Gills."

"Let's get this over with so that I can go back home to my dinner," said Nabiya, disgustedly.

Nancy walked up to the door and knocked on the doorframe with her nightstick. She did this three times while calling out to the alleged occupants in there who she was. After a few minutes, Nancy tried the doorknob. The door was unlocked. She looked over at Daniel and Jessica.

"Did either of you pick this lock?" asked Nancy, smiling at them. The looks on Daniel and Jessica's face told her, in her experience as a police officer, they didn't know anything about the lock being picked.

"No, I left my lock picking kit back at the office," said Jessica, a little worried now that she had done something wrong.

"No, I didn't touch anything," replied Daniel.

Nancy tried pushing the door open, but the mail blocked it from opening. Bob finally joined in with Nancy in rocking the door open and closed to try and dislodge the pile of mail. After a few minutes of opening and shutting the door repeatedly, the stack of mail fell over.

Nancy and Bob fell into the living room. Suddenly their noses were filled with the foul stench of a decomposing body. The blow flies that had been inside the apartment for a while flew out the open door and disappeared into the setting sun. Daniel and Jessica caught a whiff of the rotten corpse and almost gagged. Bob pulled Nancy up off of the floor and back into the fresh air outside.

"Nancy, as the duly appointed Medical Examiner for the Town of Silverton, Colorado, I hereby declare, from the stench, that the occupant or occupants of this apartment, 12A on Birch Street, are deceased and have been for some time; Nabiya, they're yours," said Bob as he ran down the stairs and stepped into his vehicle, driving off towards his home.

"Nancy, I think this is going to be a little bit messy," said Nabiya as she headed back down the steps to her vehicle.

She arrived at her vehicle and opened up what would normally be a trunk on most cars. This was a back door that allowed access to all of her equipment she might need when she found a corpse. She pulled out a pair of white, biohazard overalls and put them on; next she put a small clothespin on her nose.

Next, she grabbed several pairs of extra large latex exam gloves and another small clothespin for Nancy. Nabiya then grabbed an extra large body bag and closed the door. Nabiya then headed back up the stairs and handed Nancy the gloves and the clothespin. Nancy put the clothespin on her nose before putting on the gloves.

"Nancy, if this corpse should decide to explode, make sure that they explode on me," said Nabiya as she watched Nancy start to gag.

"Okay," replied Nancy as they went inside.

"Counselor, since you found the body or bodies, you can help us move them by getting the gurney out of the back of my car and bring it inside," said Nabiya smiling and sounding a little nasally.

"Sure, anything I can do to help, just let me know. Yours and mines taxpayer dollars at work," said Daniel to Jessica as he motioned for her to follow him to the coroner's car.

When they reached the bottom of the stairs, Jessica turned to face Daniel. Daniel could see in the setting sunlight that she was turning a slight ashen white color in her face.

"Great Buddha, Daniel, is that what a corpse smells like?" she asked, almost gagging.

"Yes, now help me with the gurney," said Daniel nicely.

They pulled the gurney out of the back of the car and took it up the stairs. Daniel and Jessica carried it into the back bedroom where Nancy and Nabiya were fighting with the bloated up body of Bob Quinest. Daniel and Jessica could see the skin had taken on a leather-like appearance.

There were dark patches on the body as Nabiya carefully zipped up the body bag. Carefully, Nabiya and Nancy put the body bag onto the gurney. Nabiya lifted up on the gurney slightly and pulled a lever on the underside. This allowed the undercarriage, which contained the wheels, to drop down. This made it easier to roll the body out of the apartment. When the body had been secured in the coroner's car, Nabiya came up to Daniel after she had taken off the overalls and gloves.

"Well, counselor, it looks like you were right. Have any idea who he is or when or how he died?" she asked as she started to fill out the report.

"I believe you will find his name is probably Bob Quinest," said Daniel as he looked over her shoulder at one of the clocks in the living room. The clock had stopped at 1938 hours. Daniel looked at all the clocks in the living room, finding that they had all stopped at 1938 hours.

"As for when he died place the date of death about a week and half ago based upon the amount of newspapers and piled up mail. As for the time, try 1938 hours."

"Were you with the person when they died, counselor?" asked Nabiya, suspiciously.

"No, but if you look at all the clocks in his apartment, you will find they have all stopped at the same time; 1938 hours. As for how he died, that's your department," said Daniel as he turned to try and face Nancy, but Jessica was pulling on his right arm.

Nabiya looked around the apartment at all of the clocks. Indeed, all of them had stopped at 1938 hours. She merely shook her head in disbelief. She assisted Nancy in opening up all the windows to help air out the place. Daniel turned to face Jessica as well as Nancy.

"Nancy, I'm assuming that this place isn't a crime scene, right?" asked Daniel.

"That's right, counselor. There's no sign of a break-in, no signs of a struggle. I will await the autopsy results."

"Then may I suggest that my private investigator here assist you with an inventory of the deceased's property?"

"Why counselor?" asked Nancy, suspiciously.

"In accordance with Colorado Revised Statutes, Title 15, Probate, Trusts and Fiduciaries, I appear to be temporarily in charge of this man's estate including all of his personal effects until such time as the next of kin has been duly notified by the authorities. The estate code also states that until the next of kin produces an attorney or a will, that the personal effects are the property of the State."

"Okay counselor. Since I don't know who the next of kin is, there appears to be no will and no attorney present, except you, who has contacted the State, which is me, I accept the help until better arrangements are made."

"Thank you, Marshal Gills. Jessica, please assist Marshal Gills or any of her duly elected representatives in this inventory. Make sure that the inventory is complete; don't miss anything."

"Sure."

As night was beginning to fall on them, Daniel headed down the stairs. Since Daniel lived in Silverton, he walked home. As the inventory continued well into the night, Jessica came across a large briefcase. She pushed in on the tabs hoping that the combination was still set. The tabs popped open and she opened the lid. There on top of all the $50's and $100's, was a receipt for the total amount of $650,000.00.

"Nancy, take a look at this," said Jessica as Nancy turned around.

"Holy crap! How much is in there do you think?" asked Nancy as she dropped her pen on the floor.

"$650,000.00 in used $50's and $100's according to the receipt. Might I ask that this money be locked up in your evidence safe at the police station for security reasons?" asked Jessica nicely.

"You'll get no arguments from me on that one."

"Don't forget to take the firearms collection either."

Nancy left the apartment with the cash and firearms. She returned a short time later and had brought along the assistant town marshal to watch over the place. Jessica went home and took a long, hot shower before going to bed around 0315 hours.

The next morning, Mary from the *Ironton Gazette* met Daniel at his office. Since there wasn't much else going on, Daniel granted her an exclusive interview. She poured herself a cup of coffee and then sat down in a chair directly in front of Daniel.

"I heard you found a corpse last night?" she asked, drinking her cup of coffee and writing in her stenographer's pad.

"Yes. My private investigator and I made the initial discovery. We called the Silverton Town Marshal, Nancy Gills and advised her to bring along the Silverton Medical Examiner, Bob Boyington and the San Juan County Coroner, Nabiya Quartez."

"So, was the stiff a client of yours that hadn't paid you for your services yet?" she asked, laughing a little. Daniel laughed with her for a second or two.

"I wish. You can help me out with the person's estate."

"How?" she asked, eagerly.

"I want you to write a story about this corpse that my private investigator Jessica Kim and I found last night. Tell the story in the same text to all of the papers in the State of Colorado. Also, see if you can get the story out on the Internet."

"Okay. Do you know who the corpse is?"

"I do, his name is Bob Quinest. I cannot tell you anything further without violating Colorado Revised Statutes, Title 15, Probate, Estates and Fiduciaries rules on me being appointed temporarily in charge of Bob's estate and personal effects."

"This sounds great, counselor."

"I'm hoping that your story will help the next of kin to contact either myself or the Silverton Town Marshal, Nancy Gills, to claim their dearly departed personal effects."

"Then I can put your name down as a point of contact?"

"Yes, by all means. Now, I have an appointment in about ten minutes, so you'll have to go."

"Thank you for the story."

"Remember, be careful what you print or I will own the newspaper."

"I will."

Mary left just as Barry was walking in to see Daniel. Lynn handed Barry the bill for Daniel's time and mileage along with Jessica's mileage. Barry took all of the paperwork and put into his small briefcase that he was carrying. Lynn showed him into Daniel's office and she closed the door so that Daniel could talk to Barry in private.

"Sit down, Barry. Although I was able to get Bill out of the federal court system, I don't think this case is over," said Daniel, flatly.

"You may be more right than you know. Is anything I tell you privileged information even though I am only paying the bill?" asked Barry. Daniel immediately detected the nervousness in his voice.

"Absolutely, your paying the bill entitles you to certain attorney/client privileges, including anything you tell me. The only exception would be if you murdered someone and you told me where the body was located. I would have to notify law enforcement. What exactly is going on?" asked Daniel as he pulled out a legal pad and started to take notes.

"At 0700 hours today, I had the usual meeting with the Board of Directors for the Baltimore Testing Center. At this meeting, I asked the Chief Legal Officer for the company, a man I detest to begin with, why the company fired Bob Quinest."

"Did they tell you why he was fired?"

"The CLO wasn't direct with an answer and that made me suspicious right then and there about the whole case. He stated that Bob was fired for some sort of ethics violations, which I suspected, but I wanted more proof. An hour after the meeting was over, I received this email instructing me to fire Bill for violating company rules," said Barry handing Daniel a copy of the email.

Daniel read over the email and set it down on his desktop.

"Did Bill violate these rules?"

"Yes, in a way. I received another email ten minutes later that instructed me not to cooperate with you, to stop paying you using company funds and to not talk with you or the authorities without the CLO or the law firm being present during the questioning. That seems a little unusual to me," said Barry, handing Daniel the other email.

Daniel read over that email and set it down on the desktop. Daniel noticed that both emails had been signed by the CLO. Daniel knew that in any court of law in the State of Colorado that those electronic signatures will stand.

"Relax, Barry. This last email has enough information in it to get your CLO in a lot of hot water. He could be charged with Obstructing Justice, Colorado Revised Statutes 18-8-102, being an Accessory to a Crime, Colorado Revised Statutes 18-8-105 and probably Intimidating a Witness, Colorado Revised Statutes 18-8-704. Linda would love this guy in a courtroom."

"Do those charges carry long sentences?"

"At least one of those charges carries a felony sentence of several years depending on the severity of the original crime."

Barry sat for a while in the chair before Daniel spoke to him.

"Do you know who your company has retained as a law firm and where they are located?"

"Yeah. The law firm that handles all of our legal compliance and legal issues is out of Kansas City, Missouri. I've personally never seen them before, but the chief financial officer keeps paying them on a monthly basis."

"Do you have a name?"

"They're called Dugan, Wainright and Lotus."

"How about an address?"

"I have their business card right here," said Barry as he pulled out their business card from his business card holder, which he kept in the small briefcase.

"Their address is 1878 E. Palatine Street, Suite #1105. Their phone number is 816-929-7474."

"Thank you, Barry and I will have this information verified. Bill made some statements to me that I need you to verify. I don't need copies of anything, yet."

"Sure, anything you need I will get it for you despite the threatening emails. What do you need verified?"

"Bill said he wrote up several informational incident reports on Bob's after-hours visitors. Do you remember those incident reports by any chance?"

"Yes, I do remember them. When I get back to the office, I will make copies of them for you and bring them by later on tonight."

"Thank you, Barry. Could you get me copies of the visitor's logs for those dates of the incident reports?"

"Sure and Bill was very meticulous about his log entries. He even went so far as to put driver's license numbers in there."

"That is the mark of an excellent security officer, Barry. Could you get me a copy of the security officer's logs as well?"

"Sure, not a problem."

"If you run into any problems, let me know. Have you checked on Bob since your company fired him?"

"I was going to ask you about that, Daniel. There appears to be quite a lot of law enforcement activity over at his residence."

"Barry, my private investigator and I made a discovery yesterday while paying a social call on Bob."

"Let me guess, judging by the coroner's vehicle and the assistant town marshal's vehicle outside of his place, he's dead."

"You're very perceptive, Barry. Keep your eyes and ears open."

"Will do and goodbye," said Barry as he left Daniel's office.

The phone started ringing. Lynn answered it and put the call through to Daniel.

"Attorney Daniel Marcos, can I help you?"

"This is Mr. Hawthorne, Mr. Marcos. Thank you for catching those awful thieves and today, I found out they are illegal aliens in this country; makes me really mad!"

"You're quite welcome, sir on catching those thieves. Be sure to tell the D.A. who's prosecuting the case against those thieves that you will testify against them. Also, make sure you tell the D.A. what kind of damages these people caused you."

"I will. I just received the Victim Impact Statement today and I need some help filling it out."

"Please, stop by my office and either my paralegal Lynn Lyons or I will assist you with that form."

"Thank you, sir. What are your rates that you would normally charge?"

"I normally charge $485.00 an hour and my paralegal charges $125.00 an hour. However, in your case, we will do it pro bono and not charge you."

"Thank you, sir. I will be in this afternoon."

"We will be expecting you; goodbye," said Daniel as he hung up the phone.

Daniel walked out to where Lynn was doing some correspondence. He saw a letterhead on the computer screen that caught his eye. The letterhead said, "APPLICATION FOR ADMISSION TO LAW SCHOOL FOR THE UNIVERSITY OF IOWA AT DES MOINES." Lynn suddenly closed the window down on the computer screen.

"Yes, Daniel?" she asked, nervously.

"Mr. Hawthorne will be stopping by this afternoon. Would you please assist him with filling out the V.I.S. in case I'm not here?"

"Sure."

"Please don't charge him. I told him we would do it pro bono."

"Okay."

"While you're at it, call this law firm in Kansas City, Missouri. Find out if they represent the Baltimore Testing Center here in Colorado. Their phone number is 816-929-7474."

"Okay," she replied as she started dialing the number.

"I'm going to lunch."

A few minutes later, Jessica entered the office.

"Where's Daniel?" she asked Lynn.

"He just went to lunch. You might find him at the usual place."

"Thanks," replied Jessica as she ran out of the office, heading for the Ironton Café.

CHAPTER 8

Daniel was just sitting down at his table inside of the local café, when Jessica found him. He asked for another menu and waited for Jessica to order her drink before he spoke to her.

"What did you find during the inventory?" asked Daniel as he sipped his drink.

"Nothing exciting until I opened up a briefcase that was sitting on the table in the living room."

"What did you find in the briefcase?"

Jessica leaned forward to whisper into Daniel's right ear.

"$650,000.00 in used $50's and $100's according to the receipt. I had the town marshal lock it up in her evidence safe along with the firearms we found in the bedroom closet."

"Good work. Can you get me a copy of that inventory list?"

"Sure, I'm going to type up my copy right after lunch. I have a copy of what the town marshal found as well. I will type it up on my computer."

"Take your time, girl. Make sure to make several copies of that inventory list. Bring my copy by the office so that I can lock it up in my safe. I want you to mail another copy of the list to yourself via Certified Mail®."

"Okay, are you expecting trouble of some kind?" she asked as she started writing down the things Daniel said.

"Not necessarily, I just want it to be done this way in case we need to establish a chain-of-custody for a court case. Could you make a third copy of the inventory list and mail it, via Certified Mail®, to Bill Berman?"

"Sure."

"While you're at it, make a complete back-up copy of your hard drive and lock up that copy in your office safe. Make a second copy and bring it to my office and I will lock up that copy in my office safe."

"Let me guess, you want me to make yet another copy, right?"

"That's right and I want you to mail it back to yourself, via Certified Mail®," replied Daniel as he was watching one of the tables at the far end of the café. There were two men sitting at it and they had been watching Daniel ever since he had come into the café.

"Will do and thanks for lunch," she replied when the food had finally arrived. The two men left at about the same time.

They ate lunch in silence, Daniel paid the bill plus tip and they parted ways. Daniel went back to his office as Jessica went to her office. Daniel walked into his office to find a gentleman, whom he recognized as one of the ones that had been watching him at the café earlier, waiting for him. The man stood up to face Daniel.

"The case you were paid for is over. Don't poke your nose around in something or someplace it doesn't belong," said the man as he left the office.

"Why, thank you very much, sir," said Daniel as he watched the man carefully after he had left the office.

"Barry called for you about twenty minutes ago," said Lynn.

"I'll give him a call. Did you have any luck getting a hold of that law firm?"

"None and I have a feeling that they really don't exist either," she said with some confidence in her voice.

"What makes you think that, Lynn?" asked Daniel as he dialed Barry's cell phone number.

"No voicemail, no rollover to an answering service, no fax machine pick-up; simply nothing. Now, I know that they are on Central Standard Time and that means it is about 1500 hours their time, but surely someone must be in the office."

The cell phone call rolled over into Barry's voicemail. Daniel left him a message and hung up the phone. He then looked up at Lynn.

"Keep trying that number until 1600 hours our time. Then, look up that law firm on the web. They may have changed phone numbers or their address or both."

"Okay."

Daniel went into his office and started doing some paperwork. Jessica came in to drop off the DVD copies that Daniel had asked her to make at lunch. She watched Lynn lock them up in the safe that was in the floor. She left at the same time Mr. Hawthorne came in with his Victim Impact Statement in hand. Lynn followed Mr. Hawthorne into Daniel's office when the phone started ringing. Lynn found out it was Barry on the line. Daniel pushed the flashing light on his phone extension.

"Mr. Hawthorne, could you wait outside of my office for just a second and please close the door on your way out," said Daniel, pleasantly.

"Yes, sir," replied Mr. Hawthorne doing exactly what Daniel had asked him to do as he left the office.

"Good to hear from you, Barry. I may have met your stumbling block today a few minutes ago," said Daniel, smiling.

"I'm very sorry that you did meet him. Well, now that you have met him, what do you think of him?"

"Charming, actually, with the personality of a mad pole cat!" yelled Daniel as they both started laughing.

"I know exactly what you mean. So, what can I do for you?"

"I have some questions."

"Go ahead."

"When you ask for legal advice from that law firm, how long does it take to get a response?"

"Depends a lot on the situation. The average is about two to four business days; why?"

"I've been trying to get in touch with them and nobody seems to be answering the telephone."

"I've had the same problem. That's why I turn over my legal requests to the CLO and he gets me the answer."

"Thanks. Do you have Bill's duty weapon?"

"Yes, I just received it back today from the FBI. It's in the safe."

"Would you pull out the magazine and tell me how many rounds are left in it, please?" asked Daniel.

Barry put Daniel on hold for about a minute before returning to the phone.

"Daniel, there are ten rounds left in the magazine; is that important?"

"It just might be. So, if he put a round in the chamber and then inserted a full magazine, he fired eight rounds. Barry, the ballistics report from the feds says they found six complete bullets and one partial bullet. Where did the eighth one go?"

"I don't know, Daniel. Do you want me to start looking around down there and see if I can find it?"

"No, is Bill going to be at work tonight?"

"Yes, he's coming in anytime now to pick up a fresh uniform and new duty gear."

"Okay. Barry, I think you might have bigger troubles than what you think. Keep your eyes and ears open. Do you have what I asked you to obtain?"

"Yes, but I cannot release it without proper paperwork."

"I'll be getting you that paperwork tonight. Can you leave it where it can be easily picked up?"

"Sure, I'll drop it off at the guard shack tonight when I leave."

"Thank you; goodbye."

As Daniel hung up the phone, Lynn knocked on the doorframe. Daniel looked up and smiled.

"Sorry about that interruption, Mr. Hawthorne, what can Lynn or I do for you on your victim impact statement for the D.A.?"

"I'm a little confused as to what kind of answer question nine is looking for."

Lynn took the V.I.S. from Mr. Hawthorne and looked it over before handing it to Daniel. Daniel looked over the question and smiled before answering Mr. Hawthorne.

"Simply put, Mr. Hawthorne, the D.A. wants to know how this crime has affected you or your farm activities, either directly or indirectly. Such examples might be, did you have to hire extra people to help protect your livestock? Have you had to spend extra money? Did you have to change your sleeping habits in order to protect your livestock? Did you exercise your horses in the morning, but now you can't because you're too tired? etc."

Mr. Hawthorne started nodding his head up and down.

"Thank you, Mr. Marcos. By the way, the other farmers in the area, like myself, are members of a neighborhood cooperative. The insurance agency we all pay into will be delivering you a check as part of the reward for the information leading to these thieves arrest. The check should be about $25,000.00."

"And thank you, Mr. Hawthorne. I will spend the check wisely."

They shook hands and Mr. Hawthorne left the office. Lynn kept on trying the phone number until around 1545 hours, Mountain Standard Time. She stopped and went through the mail that had been delivered. Lynn put official correspondence into their respective folders. She then prepared the final bills for some of the clients. She was doing some miscellaneous typing when Daniel stepped out of his office.

"Lynn, I've got some more phone calls to make, could you help me out with a few things?" asked Daniel, waiting to see her reaction.

"Sure, what can I do for you?" she asked, a little perplexed.

"Type up an affidavit for a seizure warrant. The items to be seized are listed on page six of the notes that I asked you to type up earlier this week."

"Okay and what was the other thing?"

"Tell me why this U.S. Supreme Court case was important to law enforcement and lawyers both. The case is labeled as 471 U.S. 1."

"471 U.S. 1 is a U.S. Law Reports case. I'll get started on both of them right away."

"Before you take that affidavit over to be notarized, let me look at it; okay?"

"Will do."

Daniel went into his office, picked up the phone and made a few calls. He hung up the phone as Lynn entered his office. She handed him the affidavit. Daniel looked it over and handed it back to her.

"Good work on that affidavit. Get that over to the bank and have it notarized. Deliver the affidavit to Marshal Gills or her representative and let them know that the requested documents are already waiting for them to be picked up at the guard shack."

"Okay and goodbye. I'll see you in the morning."

Daniel waited for her to leave before he went home. He read his mail, checked his email and had dinner. He went to bed around 2200 hours and was fast asleep when the seizure warrant was served. The security officer, Randy on the second shift, took the seizure warrant from Marshal Williams and handed the documents over to him. Marshal Williams locked up the information in the evidence safe.

The next morning, before Daniel woke up, the sun was starting to rise on Innovative Energy Systems, Inc. The CEO had come in early and was looking over a news report on the Internet. The news report was small, about a dead man for whom the police were trying to find the next of kin. The man's name was posted at the bottom of the picture of him; Bob Quinest. The article went on to say that if anyone had any information about him, they were to contact their local police, the Silverton Colorado Town Marshals office or Attorney Daniel Marcos, Esquire, in Ironton, Colorado. The CEO kept the screen up while he dialed Aaron's home phone number.

The phone started ringing at Aaron's place as he stepped out of the shower. He was starting to dry himself off when he heard the phone. He dried off rather quickly as he picked up the receiver after checking the Caller ID® to see who it was. He sat down on the edge of the bed as his boyfriend started to stir next to him.

"Hello Doug, what can I do for you?" asked Aaron as his boyfriend started caressing his six-pack abs.

"I know that this is one of your two days off, but I need you to come into the office. It's kind of urgent."

"Okay, I'll be there in a few minutes," said Aaron as he hung up the phone.

Before Aaron had arrived at work, Doug had already called the Silverton Town Marshals office. Marshal Gills gave Doug Daniel's phone number. As Aaron was pulling into the employee parking garage, a member of the law firm for the company was waiting in Doug's office. The law firm had sent their youngest member of the firm of Phillips, Roberts and Atkenson, Sherrie Zappatta. She was seated when Aaron entered Doug's office.

"You wanted to see me, Doug?" asked Aaron looking at Sherrie rather suspiciously.

"Sit down, Aaron. You know who Sherrie here works for, right?" asked Doug.

"Yeah, our law firm of Phillips, Roberts and Atkenson."

"I'm going to ask you a question and don't you lie to me when you give me your answer; grave consequences could become you. Did you kill Bob Quinest to get the information you gave me?"

"No, Doug, I did not kill the man. I deal in information, not murder; is he dead?" asked Aaron with a look of concern on his face.

Sherrie looked at Aaron and then at Doug and nodded her head up and down to indicate that she believed Aaron was telling the truth.

"Yes, he died about a week and half ago. I believe you Aaron. You can go back home to your boyfriend. I'll see you on Friday."

"Thanks Doug, how did you know about my boyfriend?" asked Aaron rather suspiciously.

"I make it a point to know all about my employees. This includes their sexual orientation or preference. You're, what's the term, bisexual? Your preference is for Native American, muscular males. Your current boyfriend is a Seminole Indian isn't he?"

"Yes, he is, Doug," said Aaron as he prepared to leave Doug's office.

"Aaron, how did Bob Quinest look when you left him?" asked Doug at the prodding of Sherrie.

"He was hobbling around on his right foot. I asked him about it and he said he had twisted his left ankle. I did notice a slight stench in his apartment. I offered him our medical/dental/vision plans if he came to work for us."

"Thank you, you can go now."

"Okay," replied Aaron as he left the office, this time for real.

Doug waited a few minutes before turning to Sherrie.

"Sherrie, call Attorney Daniel Marcos, Esquire. Tell him that the Law Firm of Phillips, Roberts and Atkenson has been hired to settle the estate of the late Bob Quinest by his next of kin."

Doug was silent for a few seconds before he spoke again. Sherrie was busy taking notes and making calls on her cell phone.

"Tell Mr. Marcos that we will be picking up Mr. Quinest's personal effects. When you get the money back, deposit it back into the company's general fund account. You can then sell the rest of his property and split the difference between yourself and Aaron."

"Yes, Doug," she replied as she started making more phone calls.

The phone started to ring in Daniel's office. He answered the phone because Lynn wasn't in yet. Daniel cleared his throat before speaking.

"Hello, this is Attorney Daniel Marcos, how can I help you?"

"Mr. Marcos, my name is Sherrie Zappatta; I am with the Law Firm of Phillips, Roberts and Atkenson here in Fort Lauderdale, Florida. We just found out about poor Mr. Quinest and would like to obtain his personal effects right away so that we can get them to his next of kin here in Florida."

"That's great news. Your calling me now relieves me of my duties as the temporarily appointed attorney of his estate and personal effects. Do you have any idea when you will get here?"

"Next Wednesday. Since you have handled his estate and personal effects up to this point, do you know how much in the way of personal effects he has?"

"Two bedrooms, a living room and a kitchen. Also, you will have to sign for some of his personal effects that are in lock up with the Silverton Town Marshal."

"That's fine. Can I get your fax number, so that I can fax out the release documents for you to sign?"

"That would be great. I'll sign them and fax them back to you if you want?"

"No, Mr. Marcos. Just hold onto the documents until I arrive there on Wednesday with my workers."

"Okay. Sherrie, for my records, would you give me your Florida Bar License Number? I'm not accusing you of deceiving me, but in this day and age of criminals and the fact that I am a criminal defense attorney, who sometimes gets lied to by clients, you understand, right?"

"Of course, my Florida Bar License Number is FL666934SAZ."

"Thank you very much and I will see you on Wednesday. My fax number is 970-464-7777; goodbye."

Daniel hung up the phone as Lynn walked into the office. She turned on her computer and hung up her jacket on the coat rack.

She checked the phone messages from the night before. She then walked into Daniel's office where they talked about the U.S. Supreme Court case. Daniel was pleased at how well she had picked up on the high points of the case.

"Good job, Lynn. I had a law firm out of Fort Lauderdale, Florida call me this morning about claiming Mr. Quinest's personal effects. Would you call the Florida Bar Association and find out if this bar license number I was given matches the name I was given?" asked Daniel as he handed Lynn the note he had taken.

"Will do, is there anything else?"

"Yes, look up this U.S. Supreme Court case of 467 U.S. 431 and tell me what else this case is known as in lawyer circles and what important doctrine it created."

"Okay."

Lynn went out into the outer office to start making phone calls. She made the phone calls and started looking over the U.S. Supreme Court case of *Nix v. Williams,* 467 U.S. 431. She had just hung up the phone from speaking with the Florida Bar Association and walked into Daniel's inner office.

"Her name and bar association number have been confirmed, Daniel."

"Very well, a fax should be arriving from her soon. I'll sign the release forms and when I'm done with signing them, put them into a pending file folder for later pickup."

"Will do, Daniel."

A few minutes later, Bill Berman called. Lynn put the call through so that she could look up the case Daniel had asked her about earlier.

"Bill, what can I do for you?" asked Daniel as he prepared to take notes on the questions that he had thought of yesterday to ask Bill if he called.

"I'm on suspension pending termination by HR. Barry says that all of those rules that he wrote me up for, I did technically violate. Those rules are also terminable offenses."

"Okay, hang in there. If you need a good labor lawyer, I have some connections in that area."

"Thank you, Mr. Marcos. Since I have a few days off now, I'm going to go get my stuff from Denver and get my pistol back."

"Sounds like a good plan. I do have some questions for you if you have the time right now to answer them."

"Go ahead and ask away."

"When you go on duty at the facility, do you put a round into the chamber of the weapon and then insert a full magazine?"

"Always, Mr. Marcos. Is that answer important?"

"Yes. You fired eight shots that night which I was able to confirm today. Now, the ballistics technician's report states that they only found six complete slugs and a partial seventh at the scene. The seventh slug went into the left side of the elevator door."

"Which means what? I'm a terrible marksman?"

"No, not exactly. That eighth slug hit its target, I suspect, as the elevator doors completely closed. You did hit the person that was shooting at you that night and I have a strange feeling that person was Bob."

"I see what you mean."

"You said that you could identify the two after-hours visitors that Bob had, is that correct?"

"Yes."

"Good, I have a copy of your logs and those incident reports. When will you be back from picking up your items?"

"Late Friday night probably."

"Could you come to my office Saturday morning to look at some pictures?"

"Sure, no problem."

"Thank you; goodbye."

CHAPTER 9

The toxicology results had finally come back from the lab in Durango, Colorado. The results stated that there was only a trace amount of alcohol present in the samples submitted for testing. The exact amount of alcohol found was .02. The results also showed the presence of numerous over-the-counter medicines and finally a high white blood cell count. The duty coroner put a copy of the lab results into Nabiya's in-box and went about his other duties.

Daniel left his office and drove down to Silverton. He parked outside the town marshal's office and stepped out of his car. He walked inside the town marshal's office and stood at the front counter. Nancy saw him and motioned for him to come into her office. She hung up the phone and pulled out the still sealed, manila colored envelope out of her bottom, left hand drawer that she kept locked at all times. Daniel quickly tore open the envelope and found the documents he was looking for.

"Marshal Gills, could I get a picture of these people off of their driver's licenses?" asked Daniel, pointing to the security officer log sheet entries.

"Sure, give me a little bit of time and I'll have those pictures delivered to you tonight; fair enough?"

"I'll be waiting."

Daniel left the town marshal's office and returned to his own office. When Daniel arrived, Lynn handed him the fax that had been expected to arrive. Daniel signed the fax and handed it over to Lynn to sign as a witness. She then put the fax into the temporary folder she had created. A man entered the office with a check for Daniel. Daniel signed for the check and walked up the street to the bank. He walked into the bank and went directly to the investment manager's desk.

"Mr. Marcos, so good to see you; what can I do for you?" he asked pleasantly.

"I'm here to open that 529 account that I had called you about yesterday."

"Very well, I will need two forms of identification, the check and is there anything else I can do for you?"

"Can I arrange a 5% automatic transfer from my business account to Lynn's 529 account on the 20th of every month starting next month?"

"Sure."

A few minutes later, the paperwork was done and Daniel left the bank. He returned to his office to find Lynn waiting for him. Daniel walked into his inner office and sat down at his desk; Lynn followed.

"Yes, Lynn, what can I do for you?" he asked.

"I have the answer for you. That U.S. Supreme Court case established the Inevitable Discovery Doctrine and is also known as the Christian Burial Speech."

"Excellent, Lynn, I am proud of you. For this weekend, I want you to tell me how the U.S. Supreme Court cases of *Escobedo v. Illinois,* 378 U.S. 478 and *Gideon v. Wainright,* 372 U.S. 335, changed the *Miranda v. Arizona,* 384 U.S. 436 ruling."

"Okay."

"Have you had any luck in getting in touch with that law firm, yet?"

"None; that makes me think that they are bogus, but that is just my personal opinion."

"Well, you may be right. Call Jessica; tell her to go to Kansas City, Missouri. Give her the name of the law firm and their alleged address. Tell her to see if they really do exist and tell her to do it this weekend."

"Right away."

Jessica booked her flights and hotel stay. She left the Durango airport and arrived in Kansas City, Missouri late in the afternoon. She checked out a rental car and drove to her hotel. She checked herself into the hotel and decided to wait until Saturday to start her investigation. As Jessica was having dinner, Nabiya was getting ready to go home for the weekend when her assistant entered her office. Nabiya looked up at him as he handed her the preliminary autopsy report on the newest corpse that had been brought into the morgue.

"Well, what were your initial findings on the 11 year-old, Native American male that was brought in from the reservation?" asked Nabiya.

"He was in the advanced stages of testicular cancer. I concluded that was the primary cause of death. I found cancer tissue on his left testicle, prostate gland and the cancer had moved up into his bladder."

"Excellent. I will sign off on the death certificates and you can call the family and the funeral home. Anything new in the Quinest case?"

"Nothing concrete. If I had my choice in the matter, based upon the lab results so far, I would say Septicemia was the cause of death."

"Well, you're on duty this whole weekend and not a whole lot of new corpses have come in. Why don't you pull the Quinest corpse out of the freezer and take another look at it?"

"Will do; goodnight," he said to her as she left.

Daniel closed up the office, armed the burglar/fire alarm and went home. After dinner, the Assistant Silverton Town Marshal, Marshal Williams, delivered the photos that Daniel had asked for earlier. The next morning, Daniel went to his office and waited for Bill to show up there. Bill showed up about 0945 hours. Daniel let him into the office and showed him the photos.

Bill was quickly able to identify both men from their pictures. Daniel asked if Bill was sure about the men's names. Bill then matched them up with entries he had made on his security officer log sheets by driver's license number and state. Daniel thanked Bill for coming to the office on a Saturday. Daniel locked up the door, armed the alarm and went home. Daniel had just closed the front door, when the answering service called him at home.

"Hello, this is Daniel speaking."

"Mr. Marcos, I have Jessica on the other line and she says it is important."

"Put her through."

There was an audible click on the line before Jessica started speaking.

"Daniel, I have some interesting information about that law firm."

"What did you find out already?" asked Daniel, preparing to take notes on a small notepad, with a pen attached to it, which was next to the phone.

"The address is legitimate, but the law firm that is located at that address is called Deming, Flaxe and Norman, LLC. The phone number is bogus."

"Good work, what else have you been doing?"

"I went to one of the local branches of the Kansas City, Missouri Public Library located not too far from the hotel here and searched the Missouri State Attorney General's website for the law firm name you gave me."

"What did you find out?"

"That law firm was dissolved eight years ago and it was based in Springfield, Missouri. I have the name of the assistant state attorney general who handled the dissolution case; his name is Francis Young."

"Good work; come on home."

"Will do."

"Type up your findings into a report that I can put into the file and make two copies. Bring one to the office when you get back and keep the other for yourself in a real safe place; goodbye."

Daniel hung up the phone and called Barry. Barry wasn't in, so Daniel left a message for him on his voicemail to call Daniel as soon as possible. Daniel went about doing some chores around his apartment. Barry didn't call Daniel back until early evening around 1845 hours.

"Daniel, what can I do for you?" asked Barry.

"Barry, how well do you know your CLO?"

"Well, he's not exactly a personal friend, but he came highly recommend by the CFO. The CFO and the CLO went to school very close to each other."

"Where did they go to school?"

"The CLO went to a law school in Florida, somewhere in the Fort Lauderdale area, I believe. The CFO went to a business school in Miami."

"Barry, I have a really bad feeling that your CLO and CFO are in bed with each other, if you know what I mean."

"I've suspected it for some time. However, all of my background checks have come back empty. What are they up to, anyway?"

"My guess is embezzlement. However, I think I might also throw in fraud and theft."

"What proof do you have?"

"Until I get the official report, here's the information I've gathered so far. The address for the law firm is legitimate, but the law firm that is there is called Deming, Flaxe and Norman, LLC."

"That is interesting; what else did you find out?"

"The phone number is bogus. I'm going to guess that the CLO either calls, emails or maybe texts a third party who then answers that phone at a predetermined time."

"Well, that would certainly explain the difficulty in trying to get any legal advice from them in a timely manner."

"Did your CLO tell you he was, at one time, an assistant attorney general for the State of Missouri?"

"Yes, I have that information on hand."

"Did your CLO tell you he oversaw the dissolution of the law firm you currently use?"

"No, he did not."

"Did he tell you that the law firm was actually located in Springfield, Missouri?"

"No."

"Barry, there are a lot of red flags here. I'll bet you find that the retainer checks for your alleged law firm are going to a bank account specifically set up by your CLO and that bank account is in Missouri, Iowa, Nebraska or Kansas."

"What else did you find?"

"Do you know where your CFO came from?"

"I believe his file says he came from a company in Fort Lauderdale, Florida called Innovative Energy Systems, Inc. He was their head CPA for about six years."

"That's interesting, Barry. There's a law firm out of Fort Lauderdale, Florida coming here to get Bob's personal effects. I have a hunch that law firm represents or has as one of their clients, Innovative Energy Systems, Inc. Barry, you should do a background check on that company and I suspect you will find out that the law firm is the same."

"Will do."

"I will try and find out where that phone number is located."

"Goodbye," said Barry as he hung up the phone."

Daniel hung up the phone and grabbed the business card that Barry had given him. He left his apartment and walked over a few streets to find the Silverton Town Marshal's Office. He entered the office to find Marshal Gills was working the front counter.

"Mr. Marcos, what can I do for you? Did you find another corpse?" she asked, smiling.

"Nope, fresh out of corpses today, Marshal Gills. However, could you tell me where this phone number is located?" asked Daniel as he handed her the business card.

"Why?"

"I have a hunch that phone number is to a pay phone or an unused extension somewhere in the Kansas City, Missouri area. If I'm right, then the DA will probably be calling on you to arrest and charge at least two people with embezzlement, fraud or theft."

"Okay, counselor, wait right here."

Daniel sat down in one of the few chairs that were available in the small waiting area. He was looking out the windows and had lost track of time, when Nancy returned with the printout. She handed the printout to Daniel. He looked it over, smiled and took back the business card.

"It looks like you were right, counselor. I will be eagerly awaiting the arrest warrants to overflow my inbox."

Daniel went back to his apartment and turned on his computer. He then typed into MapQuest® the address that was on the printout. MapQuest® pinpointed the address as being inside the compound fence of a place identified as the Kansas City Armory. Daniel zoomed in on the address until the buildings, fences and guard shacks were visible. Daniel exited the program and shut off his computer. He called Barry back and had to leave another message. He went to bed as the duty morgue personnel prepared for their nightshift.

The duty coroner was busy filling out paperwork, other forms and making phone calls, when the first of four lab test results came back. The first of the four lab tests being for Hepatitis A, B, C, D, E and F as well as HIV. The second set of tests was for the West Nile Virus and Mononucleosis. Both sets of tests were negative. The final sets of tests were being conducted by a lab in Durango and probably wouldn't be ready until possibly Tuesday.

He put the lab test results into Nabiya's inbox and opened up the refrigerator which contained Bob Quinest's body. He rolled the body out, washed his hands and put on gloves before beginning a very thorough examination of the entire body with a magnifying glass.

He took a break from examining the body around 0300 hours to get a cup of coffee and something to eat. He returned and found the left ankle had been shattered. As he poked around the shattered ankle, he could see bone fragments in the hole. He then saw the red streaks going up the left leg and the smell of rotting flesh was soon detected. He grabbed a small evidence container and cut a small piece of the rotting flesh off of the ankle.

He then walked the sample to the small lab in the morgue building. The duty coroner returned, pushed Bob's body back into the refrigerator and took off his gloves. He washed his hands and put some cold cream up his nose to help get rid of the smell. The duty coroner then went to the duty room to take a nap.

Daniel had just come in from his Sunday morning jog to find that Barry had called for him. Daniel started a pot of coffee and took a shower. He sat down at his kitchen table to have the breakfast he had just made. He then started reading the newspaper and to drink his coffee. Daniel reached over the table to get the telephone and after making sure the message was from Barry, Daniel called Barry.

"Good morning, Daniel," said Barry, cheerfully.

"Good morning to you, Barry. I found out where that phone number is located."

"Let me guess, it was a pay phone wasn't it?"

"Yes and according to the information I received from Marshal Gills, that pay phone is located inside the perimeter fence of a place called the Kansas City Armory at 7600 W. Ozark Road."

"I'll start the investigation tomorrow."

"I suggest that you take this information to the DA's office by close of business tomorrow. Where do the CLO and CFO live?"

"Here in Durango with me."

"Then you will have to go to the DA's office and that would be Linda in Silverton."

"I can't do that without the CEO's permission, Daniel."

"Barry, the CEO may be in on it as well; who is next in line to take the CEO's spot?"

"That would be the Chief Operations Officer."

"Can he or she be trusted?"

"They don't like me or the Board of Directors."

"Then that makes them you're best friend in this case; go get them!"

"I'll do my best; goodbye."

"Goodbye," said Daniel as he hung up the phone.

By Sunday night, the first of two special lab test results were delivered to the duty coroner. The results of the first test indicated that were was a Graham Stain Positive, as yet unidentified, bacteria present. The duty coroner pulled the body back out of the refrigerator and measured the diameter of the hole in the ankle. The hole measured .400 inches in diameter. He put the body back into the freezer.

As the day progressed, the second set of lab test results came back late that Sunday night into Monday morning. This test showed that the tissue sample submitted for testing showed signs of decomposition and gangrene infection. He put the test results into the case file for Nabiya to read when she arrived later on that Monday morning. The duty coroner did a gunshot residue test on both the hole in the left ankle and the hands of Bob. Both tests showed positive for gunshot residue. He made notes of the tests and put them into the file that had been started on Bob since he arrived at the morgue.

Monday morning arrived a little too early for Barry. He called the Chief Operations Officer and told him about all the recently gathered evidence. The COO wasn't happy about the information, but knew that by law and company policies and procedures, Barry had no choice but to go to the DA's satellite office in Durango to make a statement. Barry hung up the phone and went to the DA's satellite office in Durango to make the statement. When Barry had finished his statement, he went to work. Barry arrived at work just in time for the Monday morning meeting. The meeting was about over, when the CEO asked Barry a question.

"Barry, why is Bill Berman still employed with us?" she asked.

"If we fire Bill, like the CLO wants me to do, we would more than likely have to pay him his unemployment benefits. This is because we would be firing Bill through no direct fault of his own. So, I figured if we would have to pay him, why not pay him to work?"

"CLO, can we get some sort of confirmation on the CSO's statements?" she asked the CLO, totally evading the question asked.

"I'll call the law firm today. We should have an answer by the end of the week. I would suggest, for legal reasons, that Bill be placed on paid leave."

"CLO, I don't have the manpower to allow that right now. Besides, the CFO here is climbing all over me about overtime," replied Barry, trying to get some sort of reaction out of the CLO.

"Is this true, CFO?" asked the CEO.

"Yes, it is true. The CSO here has exceeded his quarterly allotted overtime budget by about 30K," replied the CFO, thinking quickly on his feet.

"I see. Well, for the time being, keep Bill on the payroll until I've received word back from the law firm."

"Yes, madam," said Barry, watching the whole table.

"If there is nothing else, this meeting is adjourned," said the CEO.

Everyone left the meeting. The COO followed Barry back to Barry's office; shut the door, locking it. He sat down in front of Barry.

"Barry, I hate you as well as the rest of the Board of Directors, but I also know that you have a job to do. You know that if the

CEO, CLO and CFO are arrested, there will be massive turmoil within the company."

"Yes, I am aware of that issue, however, are you ready to step up to the CEO's spot?"

"By company policies and procedures, I am required to assume the CEO's position in a case like this. My question is, are you ready to take on my position?"

"Yes, at the present time, I am ready for the position even if it's temporary."

"You know that means the CIO steps into your position and so on?"

"Yes."

"I hope, for your sake and mine, this turns out to be a wild goose chase."

"I hope so, too. If not, there will be a lot of explaining to do to the Board of Directors, the stockholders, employees and law enforcement. Have a nice day."

"You have a nice day as well," said the COO as he left Barry's office, slamming the door behind himself.

CHAPTER 10

The day wasn't starting out well for Daniel. The alarm clock failed to wake Daniel. He rolled over in bed and discovered that the time was 0700 hours. Daniel stretched out before going through his workout routine. As he left his house in Silverton, his car wouldn't start. By the time he was able to get his car started, it was already 0830 hours. He arrived at work to find three Hispanic gentlemen waiting in the outer office.

"Lynn, who are these people?" asked Daniel.

"Linda sent them over to us. They are from the Hawthorne case."

"Do any of you speak any English?" asked Daniel.

All Daniel received were blank stares to his question.

"I cannot be your public defender because I was the one who called the police on you all," said Daniel.

Blank stares were returned once again. Daniel turned to face Lynn.

"Lynn, call Juan Rivera. Put him on speakerphone. Tell Juan to tell these people I cannot be their public defender because I am a witness against them in their case."

"Right away."

Daniel walked into his inner office and sat down at his desk. He looked up at the wall that was in front of his desk and saw a picture of a dog and a fire hydrant. The saying underneath the picture seemed appropriate for how this day seemed to be going. A few minutes later, Lynn entered Daniel's office and set Jessica's report down on his desktop.

"Daniel, I need Thursday off," said Lynn.

"Let me guess, your LSAT exam?" he said as he took the report to read.

"That's right. The test is going to be given in Cortez. How did you know?" she asked, suspiciously.

"You had a screen up on the computer a few days ago for admission to a law school in Iowa, right?"

"Yes, that's right. Are you upset with me?"

"No. In fact, I think you would make an excellent criminal defense attorney. But law school isn't cheap, Lynn. I paid $101,000.00 for tuition alone and that was many years ago."

"Now I see why you charge so much money. How much do you think that law school will charge me?"

"I'm going to guess about $144,000.00 in tuition alone. Throw in the books, room and board and you're looking at more than $165,000.00."

"Whew, I see."

The phone started ringing. Lynn answered it and put Linda through to Daniel.

"Yes, Linda, what can I do for you?" asked Daniel.

"Did those nice Hispanic gentlemen I sent you, work out?"

"No, for two reasons. One, none of them spoke any English. I had to call a former client to interpret for us. Second, I was the one who called the police on them. Therefore, I cannot represent them because it is a conflict of interest."

"I thought about that after I sent them over. Did your cohort across the street represent them?"

"I believe so; he can speak Spanish more fluently than I can."

"I have your client, Mr. Berman, here in my office. He has repeatedly told me that you have already advised him on his Constitutional rights and I want a statement from him. Get your ass down here to my office and quit wasting my time," said Linda as she slammed the phone down.

"I'll be right down. Lynn," said Daniel, loudly.

"Yes, Daniel?"

"Did you receive any phone calls or messages from the answering service saying that one of our clients had been picked up for questioning?"

"No, Daniel. We had no messages or phone calls."

"Well, it appears that I have a client, whom Linda is claiming is Mr. Berman, down in her office in Silverton. I will return shortly."

"Okay."

The door opened as Daniel was preparing to leave. A police officer from the City of Durango entered Daniel's office. He looked at Daniel's driver license picture and handed him a subpoena.

"Mr. Marcos?" the police officer asked, carefully.

"Yes, Officer Gantz, I am Attorney Daniel Marcos. What is this subpoena for?" asked Daniel as he took the document.

"You are hereby directed to appear in the satellite office of the district attorney for the 6th Judicial District for case number 14-14416."

"When?" asked Daniel.

"This Thursday at 0900 hours; goodbye," said Officer Gantz as he turned and left the office.

"What a way to start the day off and it's not even 1000 hours," said Daniel putting the subpoena on his desktop in his inner office.

Daniel left his office and it took several attempts to get his car started once again. He drove to Silverton and walked into the conference room where, indeed, Bill Berman was seated along with Linda and another assistant D.A. Daniel slammed the door behind himself, set his notepad down on the conference room table and pulled out a pen from his right, upper jacket pocket. Linda went to shake Daniel's hand, but Daniel brushed it aside.

"Why are you interrogating my client without his legal representation present? You know that violates my client's 5th and

14th Amendment rights under due process. Not to mention it also violates the U.S. Supreme Court ruling in *Escobedo v. Illinois.*"

"My, my, a little grumpy this morning, aren't we," said Linda, smiling.

"No, I just haven't had a chance to pee Napalm into anyone's cereal yet, but I thought I would start with your cereal. Mr. Berman, were you allowed to make a phone call to obtain or notify your legal representation about this alleged statement as Linda calls it?"

"No, I was not allowed to make a phone call."

"Linda, are you willfully denying the accused access to their legal representation?"

"No, I was hoping Mr. Berman would cooperate with me and give me a voluntary statement."

"Are you charging my client with a crime?"

"Only if I can get a statement from him," said Linda.

"Well, he's not going to be giving you a statement."

"Then I will have to charge your client with First Degree Murder, life without parole, counselor," said Linda, confidently.

"No dice, you can't prove premeditation," responded Daniel, thinking quickly on his feet.

"Then Second Degree Murder, 20 to life, counselor."

"You would be hard pressed to prove Crime of Passion or knowingly causes the death of another does so."

"Manslaughter, 15 to life."

"No way, Linda. If you have nothing more for my client or me, we are leaving."

"Let me get the door for you," said Linda as she stood up to open the door to the conference room.

"Come on Bill, we are leaving."

Daniel and Bill walked out of the building. Daniel took Bill home and told him to lock his doors and windows, talk to no one especially the police or the press and if the police showed up to call him immediately. Daniel returned to his office to find Trooper

Davis waiting for him. Trooper Davis stood up and handed Daniel another subpoena.

"Mr. Marcos, this subpoena is for you to show up in court in Silverton as a witness to case number 14CR143," said Trooper Davis.

"The Hawthorne case, thank you Trooper Davis," said Daniel as he put the subpoena down on Lynn's desktop as Trooper Davis left. Lynn was just getting off the phone.

"If there is any possible way for me to screw up anymore today, would someone please let me know," said Daniel as he headed into his inner office, grabbing a cup of coffee along the way.

Lynn walked into his inner office and knocked on his doorframe.

"I'm not sure if this qualifies, but Nancy just arrested our client, Bill Berman. He has been charged with Manslaughter."

"That qualifies, Lynn. Call the courthouse and find out when he is going to be arraigned. Also, some days you're the dog and some days you're the hydrant. Today, I am the hydrant."

"I can see that today."

"Call the courthouse and find out when the Hawthorne case is being heard and whose courtroom will I be in."

"Yes, Daniel."

A few minutes later, Lynn put some papers on Daniel's desktop. He looked them over and found he was going to be in Judge Kyle Tillman's courtroom for the Hawthorne case. The arraignment of Bill Berman was still to be determined. Daniel looked up at the clock on the wall. It read 1130 hours.

"Lynn let's close up shop today at noon," said Daniel.

"What about our client, Bill Berman?"

"I'll visit him tonight since he's probably locked up in Silverton."

"I'm not so sure about that one. The Caller ID® said San Juan County Sheriff."

"Great, that means he's in Durango. We will start fresh tomorrow morning and don't worry, I'll pay you for the full day."

"Thank you, Daniel."

Daniel and Lynn left the office at 1215 hours. Daniel went home and sorted through his mail. He then went through his email before shutting the computer off and taking a short nap. Daniel had dinner and then drove down to Durango to see Bill Berman.

Daniel parked his car in the Visitor's parking lot, grabbed his large briefcase from the backseat and locked up his car. He made sure that he had only his car keys in his pockets. After he signed the visitor's register and presented his attorney's credentials to the jail matron, she spoke to him while she searched through his briefcase.

"Who are you here to see?" she asked, closing the briefcase back up.

"My client, Bill Berman; I am his attorney."

"Very well, I will have Mr. Berman brought to Attorney/Client room number four."

"Thank you."

The deputies escorted Daniel to the Attorney/Client room as another set of deputies put Bill into the other side of the room. Daniel and Bill picked up their respective handsets so that they could talk to each other since they were separated by a piece of Lexan®.

"Before you say anything to me, be aware that this conversation is not private," said Daniel glancing up at the jail matron who was watching them in the picket above.

"I understand, Mr. Marcos."

"Do you understand your Constitutional rights that I read you earlier or do you wish me to reread them to you now?" asked Daniel as he took out a pen from his briefcase along with a legal pad of paper.

"Mr. Marcos, would you please read me my Constitutional rights again."

"Sure thing, Mr. Berman. You have the right to remain silent. If you give up that right to remain silent anything you say can and will be used against you in a court of law. Do you understand these rights as I have read them to you?"

"Yes, Mr. Marcos, I understand those rights as you have read them to me."

"You have the right to an attorney and to have that attorney with you at all stages of questioning. If you cannot afford an attorney, the State will appoint you an attorney at no cost to you. Do you understand these rights as I have read them to you?"

"Yes, Mr. Marcos, I understand those rights as you have read them to me."

"Do you have an attorney or can you afford an attorney?"

"I have you, Mr. Marcos; until the retainer runs out, right?" said Bill, smiling.

"Having been read your rights, do you wish to make a statement to me or to law enforcement personnel?"

"I will make a statement in your office when time permits," said Bill, confidently.

"Good answer. Now, are you aware of the charge or charges against you and are you aware of the penalties of those charge or charges?"

"I have been arrested and charged with Manslaughter, Colorado Revised Statutes 18-3-104, Paragraph 1, Section A and I'm guessing that penalty is probably 20-years to life."

"Close enough, 15 to life and a felony conviction on your record. Now, I'm going to ask some basic questions. If you wish not to answer the questions I am asking, you can say I decline."

"I understand, Mr. Marcos."

"Good, let me start off by asking some basic information questions."

"Go ahead."

"Is your name Bill Berman?"

Bill looked at Daniel like he was crazy.

"Yes, the last time I checked," replied Bill, smiling as his mind started racing with thoughts of Daniel's mental competency.

"Was the social security number on the police reports and arrest warrant, or warrants, correct?"

"Yes, when am I going to be arraigned?"

"It has to be by the close of business this Friday in accordance with Colorado Revised Statutes, 16-7-204 as amended."

"What about bail?"

"Bail will be discussed at the preliminary hearing which should be fairly soon after the arraignment. I am going to try and get you moved to Silverton so that going to court for you is much easier."

"Thank you."

"To the best of your knowledge, did you recklessly kill a human being?"

"I decline to answer."

"Good. To the best of your knowledge, has anyone died recently because of your recklessness?"

"I decline to answer."

"Good answer. I'll see you at your arraignment."

"Goodbye," said Bill, hanging up the handset.

Daniel hung up his handset and left the jail. On the way back to Silverton, he called Jessica to arrange a second photo shoot at the scene of the crime. He then called Barry to schedule the time of the photo shoot to be after hours so as to not cause disruption to his business. After a good night's sleep, he woke up before the alarm clock went off. He stretched, completed his workout routine and went to work. He found Jessica was already waiting for him with her camera and other items for the photo shoot of the crime scene. Daniel soon discovered a lot of evidence boxes and file folders sitting on his desktop.

"Lynn, what the hell is all of this stuff in my office?" yelled Daniel.

"Linda knew you would want to see all the evidence she had against Bill Berman. So this morning, one of her deputy D.A.'s, the Silverton Town Marshal and her assistant town marshal were here waiting on me."

"I haven't even filed the Motion of Discovery, yet."

"Linda said don't worry about it right now. Just file it before the arraignment with today's date on it."

"That was mighty nice of her. Can you prepare those motions, Lynn?"

"Already done," she replied, handing Daniel the stack of paperwork.

Daniel took the paperwork and cleared off a small spot on his desktop to sign the paperwork. He handed the paperwork back to Lynn who notarized them. She then made copies of them for the case file and left the office. She returned a short time later.

"Daniel, aren't you due in the satellite D.A.'s office in Durango on Thursday morning?" asked Lynn.

"Yes, at 0900 hours; why?" asked Daniel, suspiciously.

"Bill Berman's arraignment is scheduled for 0945 hours this Thursday morning in Judge Bishop's courtroom."

"I can't be in two places at once. This is Linda's revenge for me peeing Napalm into her cereal earlier this week. I was going to ask for a transfer to Silverton for Bill, but that could be a problem now."

Daniel was thinking quickly on his feet about what to do before giving more orders.

"Jessica, go back to your office. If you haven't heard from me by 1900 hours, go see Barry. Make sure that you have some infrared film available and a Luminol® kit. Be creative with the Luminol® kit; think outside the box."

"Will do," she said as she left Daniel's office.

Daniel turned to Lynn.

"Let's start going through all of this stuff," said Daniel.

"Do you want me to take notes?" she asked as she grabbed a legal pad and a pen from her top, left desk drawer.

"Yes and I will dictate to you my deposition statement."

Daniel and Lynn started reviewing the mountain of evidence. When they finally finished after taking a short dinner break, it was almost 2100 hours. As they left for the evening, a car started following Daniel back to his house in Silverton.

Daniel made several different turns and noticed that the car was still following him. He looked in the rearview mirror one last time and opened up his other, smaller briefcase that was sitting next to him in the passenger's seat. Carefully, he reached inside of it, grabbing the Sig Sauer®, P-220 pistol. He eased the pistol into his lap.

Daniel could see possibly four people in the car. There were two in the front seat for sure and he could see possibly two more silhouettes in the back seat. Daniel turned another corner and called the Ironton Town Marshal's Office from his cell phone first; Marshal Beckman answered the phone.

"Thank you for calling the Ironton Town Marshal's Office, Marshal Jason Beckman speaking. How can I help you?" asked Jason.

"Marshal Beckman, are you having me followed?" asked Daniel as he turned yet another corner and started heading towards the Silverton Town Marshal's Office. The car was still following him only it was much closer this time.

"Who is this?" replied Jason, immediately on alert.

"Daniel Marcos."

"No counselor, I am not having you followed. I am by myself tonight with a couple of drunk and disorderlies. My assistant marshal is at home sick. Do you think you are being followed?"

"Yes, a car started following me when I left my office in Ironton."

Jason was already moving into action on this report from Daniel. He had accessed the San Juan County Sheriff's Department dispatch center, the Colorado Highway Patrol and the Silverton Town Marshal's Office via his computer terminal. He was typing as fast as he could with his right hand as he held the handset in his left hand.

"Does it look like a police car?"

"No."

"How many people do you see or think are in the car?"

Jason was trying to use both hands this time on the keyboard of the computer.

"I can see two persons for sure in the front seat. I think there are two more in the back seat."

Jason looked at the response times of all on-duty police officers in the Silverton area. Forty minutes for Deputy Gilda Holds to get there because she was taking care of a DUI. One hour forty-five minutes for Trooper Davis because he was on the other side of Red Mountain Pass. Only the Silverton Town Marshal was close enough to help.

"Where are you at?"

"At the corner of Highway 550A and 1st Street in Silverton. I just parked my car alongside the curb in front of the old Halsted place. The other car parked right behind me and they turned on their high beams. I think . . ."

"Daniel, don't get out of the car!" yelled Jason.

All Jason could hear over the phone as he pressed the send key on the computer terminal summoning help for Daniel, was the sound of shattering glass, yelling and gunfire before the phone was dropped by Daniel and went silent.